A VISCOUNT'S STOLEN FORTUNE: A REGENCY ROMANCE

C

ROSE PEARSON

A VISCOUNT'S STOLEN FORTUNE

Lost Fortune, Found Love Series

(Book 1)

By

Rose Pearson

A VISCOUNT'S STOLEN
FORTUNE

PROLOGUE

"*What* say you, Lord Foster, another round?" William tried to find some sort of inner strength by which he could answer, but there did not appear to be any available to him. "Capital. It is good that you are game."

He blinked furiously, trying to find the words to say that he did not wish to play again, and certainly had not agreed to it. But the words would not come. His jaw seemed tight, unwilling to bend to his will, and anything he wished to say died upon his closed lips.

Closing his eyes, the sounds of cards being dealt reached his ears. Yes, he had drunk a good deal, but he had not imbibed enough to make himself entirely stupid nor stupefied. Why was he struggling to even speak?

"And what shall you bet this time, Lord Foster?"

The gentleman chuckled, and William blinked again, trying to make him out. His vision was a little blurred and for whatever reason, he could not recall the name of the fellow he had sat down to play cards with. This was not his usual gambling den of course - he had come here with some friends, but now was sorely regretting it.

To that end, where were his friends? He did not recall them leaving the table. But then again, he could not remember if any of them had started a game with him, although it would be strange indeed for *all* of them to leave him to play cards alone. Given that this was a part of London none of them were familiar with, however, perhaps it was to be expected. Mayhap they had chosen to play in another gambling house or to enjoy the company of one of the ladies of the night.

My mind seems strangely clear, but I cannot seem to speak.

"If you wish to put everything on the table, then I shall not prevent you."

William shook his head no. The action caused him a little pain and he groaned only to hear the gentleman chuckle.

"Very well. You have a strong constitution, I must say. I do not think that *I* would put down everything on the table. Not if I had already lost so very much. You would be signing over almost your entire fortune to me."

Panic began to spread its way through William's heart. Somebody said something and laughed harshly, leaving the sound to echo through William's mind. He did not want to bet any longer but could not find the strength to speak.

"Shall you look at your cards, Lord Foster?"

William tried to lift a hand towards the cards that he knew were already there, but he could not find them. His fingers struck against the solid wood of the table, but, again, he could not find the cards.

"Goodness, you are a little out of sorts, are you not? Perhaps one too many brandies."

The gentleman's harsh laugh fired William's spirits and he managed to focus on the gentleman's face for a split second. Dark eyes met his gaze and a shock of fair hair pushed back from the gentleman's brow... but then William's vision blurred again.

"I have... I have no wish to bet."

Speaking those words aloud came as a great relief to William. He had managed to say, finally, that he had no wish to continue the game.

"It is a little late, Lord Foster. You cannot pull out of the bet now."

William shook his head, squeezing his eyes closed. He was not entirely sure what game they were playing, but he had no intention of allowing this fellow to take the last bit of his money.

"No." He spoke again, the word hissing from his mouth, as though it took every bit of strength that he had to speak it. "No, I end this bet."

Somehow, he managed to push himself to his feet. A strong hand gripped his arm and William had no strength to shake it off. Everything was swirling. The room threatened to tilt itself from one side to the next, but he clung to whoever it was that held his arm. He had no intention of letting himself fall. Nausea roiled in his stomach, and he took in great breaths, swallowing hard so that he would not cast up his accounts.

"No, I make no bet. I withdraw it."

"You are not being a gentleman." The man's voice had turned hard. "A gentleman does not leave the table in such circumstances – given that I am a Viscount and you one also, it is honorable to finish the game. Perhaps you just need another brandy. It would calm your nerves."

William shook his head. That was the last thing he required.

"Gentlemen or no, I will not be continuing with this bet. I will take what I have remaining and depart." It was as if the effects of the brandy were wearing off. He could speak a little more clearly and stand now without difficulty as he let go of the other man's arm. His vision, however, remained blurry. "I will gather up the last of my things and be on my way. My friends must be nearby."

"You will sit down, and you will finish the game."

William took in a long breath - not to raise his courage, but rather to muster his strength. He wanted to *physically* leave this gambling house for good.

"I shall not." His voice shook with the effort of speaking loudly and standing without aid. "I fully intend to leave this gambling house at once, with all that I have remaining."

Whilst his resolve remained strong, William could not account for the blow that struck him on the back of the head. Evidently, his determination to leave had displeased the gentleman and darkness soon took William. His coin remained on the table and as he sank into the shadows, he could not help but fear as to what would become of it.

CHAPTER ONE

"My Lord." The gentle voice of his butler prodded William from sleep. Groaning, he turned over and buried his face in the pillow. "My Lord." Again, came the butler's voice, like an insistent prodding that jerked William into wakefulness. The moment he opened his eyes, everything screamed. "I must apologize for my insistence, but five of your closest acquaintances are in the drawing room, determined to speak with you. Lord Stoneleigh is in a somewhat injured state."

"Injured?" Keeping his eyes closed, William flung one hand over them as he turned over. "What do you mean?"

The butler cleared his throat gently.

"I believe that he has been stabbed, my Lord." The butler's voice remained calm, but his words blunt. "A surgeon has already seen to him, but his arm may be damaged permanently, I was told."

"Permanently?" The shock that flooded through William forced his eyes open as he pushed himself up on his elbows. "Are you quite certain?"

"Yes, my Lord. I did, of course, inquire whether there

was anything the gentleman needed, but he stated that the only thing required was for him to speak with you."

"And he is well?"

The butler blinked.

"As well as can be expected, my Lord."

William nodded slowly, but then wished he had not, given the pain in his head.

"Must it be at this very moment?" he moaned, as the butler looked at him, the dipping of his mouth appearing a little unsympathetic. "I do not wish to appear heartless but my head..." Squeezing his eyes closed, he let out a heavy sigh. "Can they not wait until I am a little recovered?"

The butler shook his head.

"I apologize, my Lord, but I was told that they wish to speak to you urgently and that they would not leave until they had spoken with you. That is why I came to you at once. It appears most severe indeed."

"I see." William realized that he had no other choice but to rise, pushing one hand through his hair as the pain in his head grew. "This is most extraordinary. Whatever is it that they wish to speak to me about so urgently?"

"I could not say, my Lord." The butler stood dutifully back as William tried to rise from his bed. "Your valet is waiting outside the door; shall I fetch him?"

"Yes." William's head was pounding, and he grimaced as he attempted to remove his legs from the sheets. They appeared to be tangled in them, and it took him some time to extricate himself, hampered entirely by the pain in his head. "I am sure that, after last night, my friends must also be feeling the effects of a little too much enjoyment," he muttered aloud. "Why then-"

Shock tore through him as he suddenly realized that he could not recall what had happened the previous evening.

He could not even remember how he had made his way home. A heaviness dropped into the pit of his stomach, although there was no explanation for why he felt such a thing. Had something happened last night that he had forgotten about?

"Jefferies." Moving forward so that his valet could help him dress, William glanced at his butler who had been on his way out the door. "You may speak freely. Was I in something of a sorry state when I returned home last evening?"

There was no flicker of a smile in the butler's eyes. His expression remained entirely impassive.

"No, my Lord, you were not in your cups. You were entirely unconscious."

William blinked rapidly.

"Unconscious?"

The butler nodded.

"Yes, my Lord."

"Are you quite sure?"

The butler lifted one eyebrow.

"Yes, my Lord. The carriage arrived, but no one emerged. Your coachman and I made certain that you were safe in your bed very soon afterward, however."

Confusion marred William's brow. It was most unlike him to drink so very much that he became lost in drunkenness. He could not recall the last time he had done so. A little merry, perhaps, but never to the point of entirely losing his consciousness.

How very strange.

Shoving his fingers through his short, dark hair in an attempt to soothe the ache, William winced suddenly as his fingers found a rather large bump on the side of his head. Wincing, he traced it gingerly.

That certainly was not there yesterday.

It seemed that the pain in his head was not from drinking a little too much, but rather from whatever had collided with his head. A little concerned that he had been involved in some sort of fight – again, entirely out of character for him – he now wondered if his friends were present to make certain that he was either quite well or willing to take on whatever consequences now faced him. William urged his valet to hurry. *Did not my butler say that Lord Stoneleigh was injured? Surely, I could not have been the one to do such a thing as that!*

"I am glad to see you a little recovered, my Lord." The butler's voice remained a dull monotone. "Should I bring you something to drink? Refreshments were offered to your acquaintances, but they were refused."

"Coffee, please."

The pain in his head was lingering still, in all its strength, but William ignored it. A new sense of urgency settled over him as he hurried from his bedchamber and made his way directly to the drawing room. Conversation was already taking place as he stepped inside, only to stop dead as he entered the room. His five acquaintances, whom he had stepped out with the previous evening, all turned to look at him as one. Fear began to tie itself around William's heart.

"Lord Stoneleigh." William put out one hand towards his friend. "You are injured, my butler tells me."

His friend nodded but his eyes remained a little wide.

"I am, but that is not the reason we are here. We must know if you are in the same situation as we all find ourselves at present?"

The question made very little sense to William, and he took a moment to study Lord Stoneleigh before turning to the rest of his friends.

"The same situation?" he repeated. "Forgive me, I do not understand."

"We should never have set foot in that seedy place." Lord Thornbridge pushed one hand through his hair, adding to its disarray. Silently, William considered that it appeared as though Lord Thornbridge had been doing such a thing for many hours. "It was I who became aware of it first. I spoke to the others, and they are all in the same situation. You are the only one we have not yet spoken to."

"I do not understand what you mean." More confused than ever, William spread his hands. "What situation is it that you speak of?"

It was Lord Wiltsham who spoke first. Every other gentleman was staring at William as though they had some dreadful news to impart but did not quite know how to say it.

"My friend, we have lost our fortunes."

Shock poured into William's heart. He stared back at Lord Wiltsham uncomprehendingly.

"Your fortunes?"

"Yes. Some more, some less but a good deal of wealth is gone from us all."

William closed his eyes, his chest tight. How could this be?

"He does not know." William's eyes flew open, swinging towards Lord Pottinger as he looked at the others. "He cannot tell us either."

"Tell you?" William's voice was hoarse. "What is it that you mean? How can you have lost your fortunes? What is it you were expecting to hear from me?"

He stared at one gentleman, then moved his gaze to the next. These gentlemen were his friends, and they could have lost so much coin in one evening was incomprehensible to him. They were not foolish gentlemen. Yes, they enjoyed cards and gambling and the like on occasion, but they would never have been so lacking in wisdom, regardless of how much they had imbibed.

"Some of us do not wish to say it, but it is true." Lord Silverton glanced at William, then looked away. "We have realized that our fortunes have been lost. Some have a little more left than others, but we are now in great difficulty."

William shook his head.

"It cannot be. You are all gentlemen with wisdom running through you. You would not behave so without consideration! I cannot believe that you have all willingly set your coin into the hands of others. You would not do such a thing to your family name."

Lord Stoneleigh was the next to speak.

"I fear you may also be in the same situation, my friend." His eyes were dull, his face pale – although mayhap that came from his injury. "You are correct that we are gentlemen of wisdom, but making our way to that part of London last evening was not wise. It appears that certain gentlemen - or those masquerading as gentlemen - have taken our coin from us in ways that are both unscrupulous and unfair."

Fire tore through William as he again shook his head.

"I would never give away my fortune to the point of poverty," he declared determinedly. "I am certain I would not have done so."

"As we thought also." Lord Pottinger threw up his hands. "But you find us now without fortune, leaving us struggling for the remainder of our days. That is, unless we can find a way to recover it from those unscrupulous sorts who have taken it from us... although how we are to prove that they have done so is quite beyond me."

William took a deep breath. He was quite certain that he would never have behaved in such a foolish way as was being suggested, but the fear that lingered in his friend's eyes was enough to unsettle him. If it was as they said, then he might well discover himself to be in the same situation as they.

"I am quite sure that I cannot..." Trailing off at the heaviness in each of his friend's eyes, William sighed, nodded, and rose to his feet. "I will have my man of business discover the truth," he declared, as his friends glanced at each other. "It *cannot* be as you say. I would certainly never..."

A sudden gasp broke from his lips as the memories began to pour into his mind. He recalled why the pain in his head was so severe, remembered the gentleman who had insisted upon him betting, even though William had been somehow unable to speak. A memory of attempting to declare that he would not bet anymore forced its way into his mind – as well as the pain in his head which had come swiftly thereafter.

"You remember now, I think." Lord Wiltsham's smile was rueful. "Something happened, did it not?"

William began to nod slowly, his heart pounding furiously in his chest.

"It is as I feared." Lord Wiltsham sighed and looked away. "We have all been taken in by someone. I do not know who, for it appears to be different for each of us. Going to that east part of London – to those 'copper hells' instead of our own gambling houses - has made a difficult path for all of us now. We have very little fortune left to speak of."

"But I did not wish to gamble." Hearing his voice hoarse, William closed his eyes. Thoughts were pouring into his mind, but he could make very little sense of them. "I told him I did not wish to gamble."

"Then perhaps you did not." A faint note of hope entered Lord Wiltsham's voice. "Mayhap you remain free of this injury."

William opened his eyes and looked straight at his friend.

"No, I do not believe I am." The truth brought fresh pain to his heart. "I remember now that someone injured me. I do not recall anything after that, but my butler informs me that I arrived home in an unconscious state. If it is as you say, then I am sure that whoever I was playing cards with made certain that they stole a great deal of coin. Lifting his hand, he pinched the bridge of his nose. "Perhaps I have lost everything."

"I will be blunt with you, my friend." Lord Thornbridge's eyes were clear, but his words brought fear. "It sounds as though you will discover that you *have* lost a great deal. It may not be everything, but it will certainly be enough to change the course of your life from this day forward."

The frankness with which he spoke was difficult for William to hear. He wanted to awaken all over again, to imagine that this day was not as it seemed.

"We ought never to have left our usual haunts." Lord Pottinger dropped his face into his hands, his words muffled. "In doing so, we appear to have been taken advantage of by those who pretended to be naught but gentlemen."

"They have done more than take advantage." William's voice was hoarse. "I recall that I did not feel well last night. My vision was blurred, and I do not even remember the gentleman's face. And yet somehow, I have managed to lose my fortune to him. My behavior does not make sense, and nor does any of yours." Silence filled the room as he stretched his hands out wide, looking at each one in turn.

Lord Thornbridge was the first to speak in response.

"You believe that this was deliberate. You think that these... scoundrels... gave us something to make us lose our senses?"

"In my case, I am certain that they did." William bit his lip. "I cannot give you a clear explanation for it, but I am quite certain that I would never have behaved in such a manner. The responsibility of the title has been heavy on my shoulders for many years, and I would never have given such a fortune away."

"Nor would I. But yet it seems that I have done so." Lord Pottinger shook his head. "I cannot see any recourse."

"And yet it is there." William took a step closer, refusing to give in to the dread which threatened to tear away every single shred of determination that tried to enter his heart. "The only way we will regain our fortune is to find those responsible, and demand that they return our coin to us. I will not stand by and allow myself to lose what should see me through the remainder of my days – and to set my heir in good standing!"

His friends did not immediately reply. None answered with hope nor expectation, for they all shook their heads and looked away as though they were quite lost in fear and darkness. William could feel it clutching at him also, but he refused to allow its spindly fingers to tighten around his neck.

"We have each lost our fortune in different ways." Lord Thornbridge shrugged, then dropped his shoulders. "However are we supposed to find those responsible, when we were all in differing situations?"

William spread his hands.

"I cannot say as yet, but there must be something that each of us can do to find out who is to blame. Otherwise, the future of our lives remains rather bleak."

A sudden thought of Lady Florence filled his mind. He had been about to ask for her hand, but should he tell her about what had occurred, then William was quite certain that she would refuse him. After all, no young lady would consider a gentleman who had no fortune.

His heart sank.

"You are right." Lord Wiltsham's voice had a tad more confidence and William lifted his head. "We cannot sit here and simply accept that our fortunes are gone, not if we believe that they have been unfairly taken. Instead, we must do all we can to find the truth and to recover whatever coin we can."

"I agree." Lord Stoneleigh tried to spread his hands, then winced with the pain from his injury. "I simply do not know how to go about it."

"That will take some time, and I would suggest that you give yourself a few days to recover from the shock and to think about what must be done." Lord Thornbridge now also appeared to be willing to follow William's lead. "Since I have very little coin left, I must make changes to my household immediately – and I shall have to return to my estate to do it. Thereafter, however, I will consider what I shall do to find out where my fortune has gone. Perhaps we can encourage each other, sharing any news about what we have discovered with each other."

"Yes, I quite agree." Letting out a slow breath, William considered what he would now face. It would be difficult, certainly, yet he was prepared. He knew how society would treat him once news about his lack of funds was discovered and William would have to find the mental strength to face it. What was important to him at present was that he found the perpetrators, for that was the only way he could see to regain some of his fortune – and his standing in society.

"I should speak to my man of business at once." William dropped his head and blew out a huff of breath before he lifted it again. "This will not be a pleasant time, gentlemen. But at least we have the companionship and encouragement of each other as we face this dreadful circumstance together."

His friends nodded, but no one smiled. A heavy sense of gloom penetrated the air and William's heart threatened to sink lower still as he fought to cling to his hope that he would restore his fortune soon enough.

I will find out who did this. And I shall not remain in their grip for long.

CHAPTER TWO

"I hear you are soon to be betrothed."

Alice smiled at her friend, but Lady Florence did not smile back.

"Yes, I believe that it is to be so. My father has not yet made all the arrangements."

There was not even a flicker of happiness in her eyes or a hint of a smile on her lips.

"Whatever is the matter? I thought you liked Lord Foster?"

"He is a pleasant gentleman, certainly."

Frowning, Alice tipped her head.

"He has been courting you since near the beginning of the Season. Surely you did not expect him to do anything other than consider betrothal?"

Lady Florence still did not smile.

"I quite comprehend him, and you are quite right. He is a gentleman and is behaving as such. I ought to be pleased." Shrugging one delicate shoulder, she looked away. "Foolishly, I thought I should have a little more time before finding myself a betrothed young lady."

"I think you should be very pleased. Lord Foster is an excellent gentleman by all accounts. I have only been introduced to him, and have had no conversation whatsoever, but he appeared to be an amiable sort. He has excellent standing as a Viscount and, I believe, an exceptional fortune."

Lady Florence nodded but dropped her gaze to the floor without saying a word. Lady Florence had always been a quiet young lady and tended towards personal introspection, never truly being open with Alice about her feelings on any particular subject.

"We have been friends for a long time, have we not?" Alice kept her voice soft, placing a hand on Lady Florence's arm. "We do not often speak of our hearts, but I do want you to know that I am ready to listen, should you have anything more to say."

Lady Florence immediately looked up.

"What do you mean?"

There was something else winding through Lady Florence's voice, but thus far Alice could not make out what it might be.

"I did not mean anything by the question. It was only to state that, should you have something more you wish to express, if there was some other reason that you did not wish to become betrothed to Lord Foster, then I would be more than willing to listen without judgment or astonishment." Shrugging her shoulders, Alice gave her friend as warm a smile as she could manage. "That is all."

"No, there is nothing." A thin-lipped smile bit at Lady Florence's mouth, but it did nothing to warm her eyes. "You have heard the truth of it. I did not wish to become betrothed so soon, but this is my second Season, and I should have expected as much from my father. He thinks very highly of Lord Foster."

"As is to be expected. You are very lucky indeed, my dear friend. Not all young ladies are as fortunate as you in finding a gentleman who is eager to marry them, so soon into their second Season."

This, in turn, sent a flare into Lady Florence's eyes.

"You do not mean to say that you have any concerns for yourself, my dear Alice?" Suddenly, the conversation was turned from Lady Florence to Alice's situation. "The Season has only just begun. You cannot expect to find a husband as quickly as I have done so. My father's determination that I should wed as quickly as possible accounts for Lord Foster's interest. Your father, it seems, has no such concern."

Alice smiled softly to disguise the pain that ripped through her heart.

"Yes, you are quite right in saying so." She had not yet told Lady Florence that her father had stated that she would *have* to find a husband come the end of the Season, else be sent to an older aunt living in the far south of England, to act as her companion. It did not help that her father did very little to encourage her, nor to aid her in finding a match. And her mother was quite taken up with her youngest daughter who was, of course, the beauty of the family, and therefore worth much more effort in terms of making a good match. *She* was the one expected to make an excellent match, whereas Alice, on the other hand, was expected to make very little of herself. "I hope I shall soon have the same good fortune as yourself." She linked her arm with Lady Florence, and they began to wander through the drawing room. "Mayhap there shall be a gentleman here this evening who will catch my attention!"

Lady Florence smiled, her eyes clear. It seemed that in only a few moments she had forgotten about her betrothal to Lord Foster and was now thinking solely about Alice.

"You may not think it, my dear friend, but you are very beautiful. I am sure that there will be at least one gentleman present who will be eager to be in your company."

Alice shook her head.

"You need not pretend, Lady Florence. I am aware that I am a little plain. I do not have my sister's hazel eyes that swirl with green and brown. Unfortunately, I am left with my father's grey eyes, which appear clouded and shadowed no matter how I am feeling. Nor do I have her slim figure and beautiful golden curls. Again, my father has blessed me with his dark hair that does not like to sit in curls and insists on remaining quite straight."

Lady Florence did not laugh but instead turned to look up at Alice.

"You may laugh in an attempt to convince me that you are quite plain and are never to be looked upon by a single gentleman, but you ought not to believe that. Your smile turns your eyes to silver and your hair is as dark as a raven's wing. You have a beauty that is all your own."

Then why is it that I have never so much as had a single gentleman pay the smallest amount of attention to me?

"You are very sweet, my dear friend. And it is kind of you to be so encouraging. Mayhap it shall be that you are proven correct." In truth, Alice had very little idea of what she would do if she were not able to soon find a suitor. It was only the start of the Season, but it would go quickly, and she might find herself at the end of it in the same position that she stood in at present. Throwing off such depressing thoughts, she drew in a deep breath, finding her attention caught.

"Look, there is Lord Foster now." Alice did not point to him but followed him with her eyes as he walked across the room. "Perhaps we should speak to him this afternoon."

"I suppose I must."

Lady Florence lifted her chin and sighed heavily, as though speaking to her gentleman was a burden, something Alice still did not understand. From her point of view, Lord Foster was a very handsome gentleman with an excellent character. From what she remembered, his eyes were a very dark green, reminding her of the waves of grass at her father's estate, when the sun was just beginning to dip towards dusk and casting shadows over the grounds. His dark hair and eyebrows added a little more shadow to his normally cheerful countenance although today, she noticed, it was a little lacking. His smile came and went at quick intervals, as though he were not truly as cheerful as he appeared. It did not surprise her that Lady Florence had no comment to make on this particular expression. Yet again, her friend seemed dulled and upset by the fact that she would soon be betrothed to Lord Foster.

Glancing toward Lady Florence, Alice was surprised to see that her eyes were not on Lord Foster at all. Instead, she appeared to be considering another gentleman entirely. A note of surprise struck her heart. Could it be that her friend considered another gentleman to be a more suitable match than her suitor? That would not be altogether surprising, Alice considered, for Lady Florence had never been permitted to express an interest in any gentleman whatsoever. Her father had told her whom she was to accept.

If that is as things stand, then she will tell me of such a thing in her own time, I am sure.

"Look, he is coming to join us."

It seemed that Lady Florence would not be able to put

off her meeting with Lord Foster any longer, for he was now making his way to join them. Alice had not often had an opportunity for conversations with the gentleman, given that he had always been eager to spend time, or dance with, Lady Florence. Perhaps now, she considered, she ought to leave her friend to speak with the gentleman so that they might have a little more privacy. As if she had been able to read Alice's thoughts, Lady Florence's hand grasped her fingers tightly. The pressure on her hand was a little surprising, and Alice did her best not to jerk visibly.

"My dear Lady Florence." Bowing low, Lord Foster reached out and took Lady Florence's hand for a moment. "And Miss..."

He seemed to forget her name and a flush colored his cheeks.

"Miss Lawrence."

Lord Foster nodded, as though that was the exact word he had been searching for.

"Yes, of course, Miss Lawrence. Good afternoon to you." His green eyes did not linger on her for long but instead went directly to Lady Florence. "I hope you are well?"

"I am." Lady Florence's voice held very little warmth. "And you?"

At this, Lord Foster hesitated. His eyes went to the left and the right, as though somehow, he would be able to find the answer there. Noting this, Alice glanced up at her friend. Was there something wrong? Or was Lord Foster hoping to ask the lady to marry him at this very moment whilst she herself looked on?

"You find me a little out of sorts, my dear lady." Again, Lord Foster continued to speak directly to Lady Florence, without so much as looking in Alice's direction. "It is nothing too severe, I hope, but I find myself a little disturbed. I shall, I believe, have to speak to your father."

Alice's eyes widened a little at Lord Foster's words. Whatever the matter was, to speak of being disturbed did not put her in mind of betrothal. A glance towards her friend told her that Lady Florence was thinking the same thing, for her eyebrows were knotted together.

"I do hope there is nothing of grave concern?"

Lady Florence's voice was a fraction higher.

Again, Lord Foster hesitated, and Alice's eyebrows shot towards her hairline. Something, it seemed, was indeed the matter.

"I shall not speak of it to you at present, for I do not wish to upset you in any way." Lord Foster tilted his head and smiled warmly, although it did not last for more than a brief moment. "Tell me, is your father present this afternoon? I shall make an arrangement to speak with him as soon as possible, if he is present."

"He is not present." Lady Florence's fingers tightened on Alice's. "However, I can speak to him when I return home and inform him that you have an urgent wish to meet with him?"

"I would be very appreciative of that. However, I came to speak with you. In the hope that any bad news would not have any bearing on our present situation. I am afraid I cannot go into further detail at this time, but I must beg of you, Lady Florence, that, whenever you hear of this particular news, you will not turn from me. It is a matter which will become clear in time. All will be returned to the position it once was. It is only a matter of time, and I must beg of you to give that to me."

Alice blinked, all too aware that she ought to step away and allow Lord Foster to continue his conversation with

Lady Florence in private. But she felt too much confusion to do so and, besides which, her friend still held her fingers tightly. Whatever this was, it sounded very serious indeed, and Alice found herself a little concerned for her friend. Lord Foster did not lift his eyes from Lady Florence, seeming to silently beg her to respond.

Alice squeezed Lady Florence's hand, urging her to say something at the very least, rather than just stand there silently. This seemed to startle Lady Florence for she jumped visibly, looked directly towards Alice, and then back towards Lord Foster again.

"You find me at quite a loss, Lord Foster. I do not know what I ought to say, for I have no knowledge as to what this concern might be."

"I quite understand." Again came Lord Foster's smile, but it did not touch his eyes. "You will know it soon enough. I dare not tell you here for fear of what your reaction might be. It will be a shock, Lady Florence, but I pray that once it has passed, you will have an understanding that this situation is not of my own doing. I pray that you will see a brightness in the future as I fight to regain what has been lost. I can only hope that you will be willing to wait."

At that very moment, someone came to speak directly to them, and Lady Florence and Alice were left to stand together, staring at Lord Foster as he moved into conversation with this new gentleman.

Lady Florence had not yet let go of Alice's fingers.

"Whatever can such a thing mean?" Alice whispered as Lady Florence stood there, her jaw a little slack. "Florence, are you quite alright?"

Her concern seemed to tug Lady Florence out of her stupor as she turned wide eyes towards Alice.

"Whatever can he mean?" she asked, in such a harsh

tone that it took Alice every ounce of strength not to hush her friend. "What he said is entirely incomprehensible and yet I have such a great sense of fear that I do not think I shall be able to remove it from me until I can hear what my father has to say. I wish to go home at once and demand that he speak to Lord Foster this very day!"

"I understand that you wish to do so, but you must not." Alice did her utmost to keep her voice calm whilst inwardly questioning everything Lord Foster had said. "We must linger here until the soiree is over. You cannot draw attention to the situation. It would only make things worse, for you would catch everyone's attention by your sudden departure, and rumors might quickly spread thereafter."

Lady Florence stared at Alice as though she were making very little sense.

"Come in search of some refreshment." Ignoring the gentleman who had come to speak with them but was, at present, in conversation with Lord Foster, Alice slipped her hand through Lady Florence's arm and began to walk away, murmuring reassurances to her friend. Her mind continued to hound her with questions. Whatever was troubling Lord Foster, it sounded very grave indeed, and Alice could only pray that Lady Florence was not about to become injured in any severe way. She had to hope that the truth would soon be revealed – for everyone's sake.

CHAPTER THREE

"*L*ord Bothwelll." Clearing his throat, William put both hands behind his back and looked directly into the face of the gentleman who would decide his future. "Thank you for seeing me."

"You have put my daughter into quite the state." Lord Bothwell did not appear at all amused. "She has been almost inconsolable since her arrival home from the soiree yesterday afternoon. I told her that there was nothing of great concern, but now, from your expression, I believe that there is, in fact, something for me to be concerned about. Is it a serious matter?"

"It is." There was no point in pretending otherwise. William had come here with the full intention of being entirely open and honest with Lord Bothwell. "A few days ago, I found myself in a part of London that I had never set foot in before. My friends and I went together at the invitation of another acquaintance, Lord Gillespie. Unfortunately, that evening did not end pleasurably." Seeing Lord Bothwell's eyebrows lift, William quickly tried to explain. "When I awoke the following morning, my friends and I recalled very little of what had taken place. We were all in differing situations, but the truth is, Lord Bothwell. we were all stolen from."

The gentleman's eyebrows lifted sharply.

"You were attacked."

"In one respect, yes." His hand reached up to rub through his hair, as though he could still feel the hand sweeping hard at his head. "It seems, Lord Bothwelll, that we were incapacitated in some way. My friends and I have found ourselves lacking a good deal of funds. They have been taken from us by the most unscrupulous of means." His words were coming quickly now, as William did his best to not only explain but to reassure Lord Bothwell that he would soon recover the situation. "Given that my friends and I were all in different gambling houses and the like, it has proven difficult to find ourselves back to a path of understanding. However, we are all singularly determined to find the culprits behind these attacks so that we might recover our fortunes. It will take a little time, but I am certain of success."

Lord Bothwell's eyebrows dropped as his eyes narrowed slightly, looking hard at William. Silence filled the space between them. William shifted from one foot to the other, his hands clasped behind his back as he waited for the gentleman to reply. The urge to say more and to explain himself further pressed down hard on him, but with an effort, he remained stoic. It seemed like an age before Lord Bothwell replied.

"Do you mean to say, Lord Foster, that you have no fortune?"

"I have wealth, Lord Bothwell." William tried his utmost to explain. "As I have said, it has been taken from me, but I am determined to get it back. I am not the sort of fellow who throws away his fortune for the sake of a spot of gambling or a little game of cards!"

Lord Bothwell looked away. Again, silence filled the space, and William's heart began to drop low. From the gentleman's expression, it did not seem that he was at all understanding.

"You have no fortune, Lord Foster." Lord Bothwell spoke slowly as if he wished to understand the present situation entirely. "You say you have had it stolen from you, but the truth seems to be that you have lost it through gambling, not through theft."

William shook his head.

"No, that is not so. I was given something that made me —"

"I will not have excuses!" Lord Bothwelll suddenly rose from his chair in a thunderous cloud of ominous fury. "If you have lost your fortune, then you shall not be betrothing yourself to my daughter!"

"As I have said, I did not lose it. It was taken from me." His voice sounded weak against Lord Bothwell's wrath.

"So you say, but I am afraid I cannot quite believe that. For all I know, you could be making up this excuse to continue with your betrothal to my daughter in the hope of gaining her dowry! Do you really think I would be so foolish as to permit my daughter to marry a gentleman who lost his entire wealth on an unwise game of cards?"

The air between them crackled with ire, and William saw in the darkness of Lord Bothwell's eyes that there was nothing he could do or say which would convince him otherwise. He appeared quite determined to believe that everything William said was nothing but a lie and that he had lost his fortune by his own foolishness.

I cannot blame him for that. Even to my own ears, my explanation sounds ridiculous.

"Then you will not permit me to offer my hand to your daughter."

Lord Bothwell threw out both hands.

"You should not need to *ask* me such a thing. No, Lord Foster, you will *not* be permitted to wed my daughter." His words dripped with irony. "Furthermore, your courtship has now come to an end. You may greet her, yes, but there will be no continuing of this familiarity between you. Do I make myself quite clear?"

William nodded. He had nothing left to say. Lord Bothwell turned his head, making it plain that he was dismissing William without another word. Not speaking even a farewell, William left the room, turning on his heel sharply towards the door.

Striding from Lord Bothwell's house, he did not have an opportunity to speak with Lady Florence herself, having no doubt that her father would speak to her of what had occurred - and despite his veiled urgings that she consider the matter fairly and give him the time and opportunity to rectify it, William was not certain that she would urge her father to permit her to wait for William's endeavors, as regarded his fortune. The truth was, he had often felt a lack of interest from Lady Florence, but that had not mattered since her father had agreed to the match. He had believed that her affection for him would come in time, but now there would not be any opportunity for it to grow. There was to be no future for himself and Lady Florence. All the plans he had built up in his mind about what lay ahead for him were now completely shattered. There would be no marriage to a gentleman's daughter, no happy future where he and his wife would bring up their children at his estate.

Instead, he would be left to struggle through the next few years, trying desperately to make enough money to keep his estate from falling into disrepair. Everything he loved would have to be given up.

William stopped short as he reached his carriage. The door was held open for him, but he did not immediately step inside. Would Lord Bothwell now tell others in society of his troubles? He had tried, thus far, to keep his misfortune secret, but by speaking to Lord Bothwell, he had risked everything he had worked to hide so far. He had not expected such a forceful reaction from the gentleman he had thought soon to call father-in-law. He had assumed, wrongly, that Lord Bothwell would be willing to listen, to be understanding and considerate. Instead, he had refused to give William even a few more minutes of his time. His answer had been swift and forthright. There could be no match between William and Lady Florence, not when his fortune was so severely diminished.

William dropped his head as a huff of breath escaped him. He had to pray that Lord Bothwell would not tell anyone else about what he had heard from William. There was no guarantee, however, that the gentleman would not do so - in fact, it was more likely that he would speak to as many of his acquaintances as he could, in an attempt to protect the young ladies of London from William's clutches.

"My Lord?"

It took William a moment to realize that his footman was still waiting for him to step into the carriage. Clearing his throat, he stepped up, sitting back against the squabs as he realized that he would soon have to give up such things as this. If he had not the money to pay his staff, then they would have to be severely reduced in number. That was not something he wished to do, but something he would *have* to do – and he might even be forced to sell his horses and, with that, near all of his carriages and phaetons.

Misery filled his thoughts as his carriage pulled away from Lord Bothwell's townhouse.

Perhaps it would be better for me to return to my estate rather than linger in London.

After all, what was here for him? Once Lord Bothwell told everyone in society about his difficulties, then he would have very few friends here. People would do all that they could to avoid him. He would have no opportunity to court any young lady, nor think about making any sort of proposal. None would so much as glance at him, not when they knew he was so poor.

"Then my only hope is to regain my fortune."

Speaking aloud, William kept his eyes wide and pointed forward, trying to build determination into his heart. Thus far, he had very little idea of what he was meant to do, as regards finding the culprit, but he was willing certainly to try. After all, he realized it was the only thing that would aid him in his wish to return to society's good graces, and a more certain future.

"You APPEAR to be a little lost, Lord Foster."

"I am not lost." William glanced over at his friend. "How do you fare, Lord Wiltsham?"

"I am struggling." Lord Wiltsham shook his head. "I have not yet made any endeavors into resolving my situation. I am attempting to come to terms with just how much I have lost, but that seems to be a constant struggle. At this point, I do not think I can even afford to return to my seat! I have not yet let my servants know of it, but I shall soon have to encourage them to find other employment since I cannot pay their wages for more than another month or so."

"You shall keep none at all?"

William's eyebrows lifted. At least he was able to keep on some of his servants.

"I believe that the only people I can keep on would be my butler – who will double as my valet - the housekeeper, two maids, and a couple of footmen. And that may only be for another few months until my coffers run out entirely."

"You will have gained back your fortune by then." Trying to speak confidently, William clapped his friend on the shoulder. "I am certain we shall expose these ruffians for what they are."

Lord Wiltsham looked towards him.

"You are truly convinced that it is a small group of men who work together to achieve such an end? They deprive gentlemen of their fortune, one way or the other, believing that there is no recourse for them to regain it?"

"I am quite convinced." William spoke with a confidence that did not envelop him entirely. Then a sudden idea came to him, and he grasped his friend's arm. "And surely that should be our first consideration! Speaking with the gentleman who encouraged us to go to that part of London in the first place."

"Lord Gillespie?" Lord Wiltsham frowned. "But he is a gentleman known to all of us. He is of good character and all of society is engaged by him. I cannot see him doing anything unscrupulous."

"And maybe that is precisely how he has done this. Given that we believe him to be of good character, he may be using that to hide despicable deeds."

"For what reason?"

No immediate idea came to William's mind.

"I could not say. Lord Gillespie is only an acquaintance, but it may be that he struggles with his own coffers. Perhaps this way he can make certain that his fortune is always replenished."

"Or he may have had an excellent evening in one of those gambling houses and sought to encourage his acquaintances to attend also. It may be nothing more than that."

"It may be entirely innocent," William agreed. "But the only way we will discover the truth is to ask him directly."

Lord Wiltsham nodded slowly.

"Very well. Is that who you have been searching for?" He smiled as William's eyebrows lifted in surprise. "You have been looking across the ballroom for many minutes, barely catching my eye for a single moment."

William immediately closed his eyes as if he wished to hide them from his friend.

"Foolishly, I have been looking for Lady Florence."

When he opened his eyes, Lord Wiltsham was looking back at him in confusion.

"Why should such a thing be foolish? I thought you wished to marry the lady."

"I did... I still do. But her father will not permit me to pursue her any longer."

Lord Wiltsham's smile dimmed.

"And might I ask if his reason for doing so was due to your financial difficulties at present?"

William nodded and ignored a slight tightness in his throat. He had thought Lady Florence to be the most beautiful of young ladies from the very first moment that he had set eyes on her, and had been eager to make her acquaintance. Everything had been going very well indeed, and he'd had every intention of proposing to her, but now that would no longer be a reality.

"He would not listen to you then?"

"No, he would not." The smile he put back on his lips was strained. "He stated that without my fortune, I could not even court his daughter. I do not think that I will even be permitted in her company for long! I am afraid, however, that her father will tell the rest of society about my circumstances, and all will be lost. Thus far it was only the six of us who knew the truth – but now, however, there are seven. Lord Bothwell could easily say something which would not only injure me but would also injure the rest of you."

"That is concerning indeed. Then it is he you are looking for, yes?"

Again, William shook his head.

"No, it is not he. It is Lady Florence that I seek. Yes, her father has rejected me, but she has not. You may call me foolish, but I begged her to consider me, even though what news I had to share was not pleasant. I have not yet heard from her whether or not she will be willing to do so. If she gives me even the smallest hope, then I shall return to her father and beg him to reconsider." Lord Wiltsham did not respond. A frown marred his brow still, but he did not speak. "You think me unwise."

His friend looked over at him.

"Would you be very angry with me if I said that I did?"

"Why should you say such a thing? There was a connection between the lady and myself from the very moment that I saw her."

"Mayhap you consider that there was such a connection, but perhaps she does not. I believe that if you do this, you will find yourself in even deeper sorrow than you are at present. You ought not to be pursuing her when her father has made his decision clear. Leave the matter as it is. Concentrate on finding the perpetrator behind the removal of your fortune and, mayhap, you will be granted the opportunity to have her in your arms again."

"I cannot do that, for then she might have already taken up with another. I know that her father is very eager indeed to have her married off, and I shall be much too late!" William's heart beat a little more quickly as he thought of a life without Lady Florence, and yet the more he attempted to hold onto that idea the more it felt as though it were slipping from him. "I do not want to be without the lady."

"You may have to be." Lord Wiltsham held up both hands. "I can see that you may well be irritated with me for stating it so plainly, but surely you can see the wisdom in my words?"

The truth was that William *did* see it, but he had no willingness to accept it. Biting his lip, he continued to look around the room to search for the lady but had no luck.

"I could always speak to that friend of hers, the one she is so often in company with."

Lord Wiltsham left out a long sigh that told William exactly what he thought of such a suggestion.

"That way, I am not speaking directly to Lady Florence, but I *am* speaking to her friend, so that I might find out whether I have any hope. Surely you cannot disagree with that?"

"I believe that you are going to be greatly disappointed."

Waving a hand in William's general direction, he arched one eyebrow, as William nodded fervently, convincing himself that this was a very wise idea indeed. It seemed almost providential, then, that his eyes immediately fell upon the young lady in question. Quite certain that course of action was the right thing to do, he hurried towards her, leaving Lord Wiltsham to watch on, shaking his head.

His heart pounding a little more quickly as he approached the young lady, William cleared his throat and lifted his chin a notch. It seemed to take her a few moments to realize that he was coming with the intention of speaking to her, for she glanced at him and then looked away, only to turn her head towards him again.

"Good evening." He offered her a short, sharp bow which seemed to catch her a little off guard, for she stepped back with wide eyes and did not immediately return with the gesture with a curtsey of her own. "Miss..."

For what was the second time, William realized that he could not recall the young lady's name. This seemed to frustrate her, for she frowned hard, her lips pulling downwards.

"Miss Lawrence."

William nodded quickly.

"Yes, Miss Lawrence, of course." He made to bow for a second time, realizing just how poorly he had behaved. He should have given it a little more thought before he approached her. "Forgive me, I am in something of a state. I was sure that Lady Florence would have spoken with you about the matter. She will have heard it from her father by now."

"You are quite mistaken, Lord Foster." Miss Lawrence kept her eyebrow lifted but folded her arms lightly across her chest. "I have not yet seen Lady Florence this evening. In fact, I have been a little concerned as to where she might be."

Her eyes searched his as though she suspected he was the cause of her friend's absence. And as much as he wanted to protest, William realized he could not do so. He might very well be the reason that she was absent from the ball this evening.

"I see."

A little uncertain of what he ought to say next, William bit his lip. Ought he to explain the situation to her? Grimacing. he looked away.

"Is there something the matter?" Miss Lawrence's grey eyes were filled with nothing but steel. "What is it that you have done?"

The accusation in her voice burned him, and it took William a moment to compose himself. Recalling that she had been present when he had spoken to Lady Florence the previous day, William took a breath, then smiled briefly.

"You will remember that I begged Lady Florence to give me the opportunity to explain, once her father had spoken to her, but Lord Bothwell has made it clear that we are no longer betrothed." A knot in his stomach, he lifted his chin. "I must hope, perhaps beyond all reasonable consideration, that she will give me further opportunity. Even if her father declares me unsuitable, surely there must be a part of her that continues to consider me? Once I have regained my fortune, I –"

Miss Lawrence drew back as though she had been stung.

"You have lost your fortune?" she repeated as her eyes flared wide. "All of it?"

A little needled, William took in a sharp breath and looked away.

"I did not come here to give you explanations. I came here to ask if you would speak to Lady Florence and ask her whether or not she would be willing to wait for me."

"To wait for you?"

William threw up his hands.

"It is a little irritating, Miss Lawrence, that you continually repeat the words I have only just said to you. Yes, I wish very much to know whether or not she will wait for me to regain my fortune, which was stolen from me. I might add. It was not lost by my own foolishness - of that, I can assure you."

For some moments, Miss Lawrence said nothing, merely staring back at William, as if she could not comprehend what he had told her. The music and the laughter continued all around them, but William's attention was solely on her, waiting for her response, and he tapped his foot impatiently when she did not speak.

To his horror, the only thing that eventually came from Miss Lawrence was a snort of either laughter or ridicule. She immediately held up both hands and shook her head frantically as though to beg him to forgive her for her outburst, but the mirth in her eyes remained. They flashed with bolts of lightning running through them, and William responded with thunderous anger.

"Yet again I find myself in a situation where I am to be mocked. I ask you one simple thing and you will not so much as even consider it!" Seeing her open her mouth, he held up both hands and shook his head, his jaw tight. "Pray forgive me for having thought you might be willing to do so."

He turned sharply, meaning to walk away, only for a soft hand to catch his. When he turned again, she dropped her hand quickly and lowered her eyes.

"I beg your forgiveness for my response, but I must tell you truthfully that there is nothing you can say or do that will *ever* convince Lady Florence to disobey her father. It is quite unheard of. Even if she should consider it, it is not something she would ever do. Forgive my laughter, it was not directed towards you but rather at the thought of Lady Florence disobeying her father."

The anger he had felt upon hearing her laughter

quickly faded into despair. It seemed that he was not to have any opportunity to regain his association with Lady Florence.

"She will not wait for me then. She will not wait for me to recover my fortune and present myself once again to her father."

He dropped his head, but not before he caught the way that her eyes flickered. Her lips pursed gently, but she did not say anything. It was as though there was something within her that she wanted very much to express but did not feel able to. William could not blame her, given the fact that he had spoken to her in such anger.

"I will speak to her, of course, but I would not hold out any hope." Miss Lawrence's voice was softer now, as though she saw his pain and was sorry for it. "It seems that you have been through a great deal already and now to lose your attachment to Lady Florence must make your struggle all the greater."

William said nothing. Instead, he lowered his head and rubbed one hand over his eyes. Miss Lawrence had gone from an unwilling listener to a sensitive, caring sort, it appeared, but William had no willingness to open up to her and tell her the truth about his current despair. There was no need for her to know the depth of it. The fewer who knew of his position, the better.

"Then it seems as though all hope is lost." His mumbled words were as much to himself as they were to her. "Whenever you next speak to Lady Florence, as I'm sure you shall about this situation, pray do not think too unfavorably of me." He did not so much as glance at her, putting out one hand to her. "I did not willingly lose my fortune. I did not willingly step into poverty. It has been taken from me and I shall do everything in my power to regain it, even though it seems I shall lose the woman I was to marry, as well as my social standing. I am sure that Lord Bothwell will waste no time in telling all of society about my circumstances." He could not keep the note of bitterness from his voice. "I pray that you will think a little well of me, Miss Lawrence, and that something of what I have said will have made an impact on you. Good evening."

So saying, he stepped away, leaving Miss Lawrence to look after him, no doubt wondering what it was that he had meant by those final few words.

William grimaced to himself. She would not have to wonder for long.

CHAPTER FOUR

"Good afternoon, my dear friend."

Alice smiled warmly as she reached out one hand towards Lady Florence. Yesterday's conversation with Lord Foster was not one that she had been able to forget, but Alice was determined that she would not discuss it until Lady Florence herself chose to speak of it. Her friend was a little paler than usual and she did not smile when Alice greeted her which, in itself, was most unusual.

"My dear Alice." Lady Florence took her hand, squeezing it hard. "How grateful I am that I have found you this afternoon."

"I am glad to see you also," Alice replied, truthfully. "My mother insisted that she and my *darling* sister Henrietta take a walk in Hyde Park. I was only useful for a short while in making certain that Henrietta had company, but she has soon gained acquaintances and I was no longer useful."

With a rueful smile, she inclined her head lightly over her shoulder and saw Lady Florence's eyes turn to where

Alice knew her mother, Lady Blackford, and her sister were still talking at length to the two gentlemen and the lady who had come upon them in Hyde Park. They had not even noticed that Alice had stepped away.

"My mother is present also." Lady Florence smiled briefly, but it did not touch her eyes. "She is conversing with Lady Kellington and, no doubt, informing them that I am no longer closely connected with Lord Foster."

"Yes." Alice pressed her friend's hand gently. "I am sorry for that."

Lady Florence's eyes widened.

"You are aware of the situation?"

"Yes." Quickly, Alice explained. "I spoke with Lord Foster last evening. He begged me to inform you of his eagerness to speak with you again. I believe he hoped that you would find it in your heart to wait for him still, even though he is practically penniless."

Lady Florence shook her head.

"My father will not hear of it." Alice noted that there was no particular disappointment filling Lady Florence's voice. "Lord Foster has lost his fortune and thus I cannot tie myself to him. It would lead to an impoverished life, and I cannot do such a thing as that."

"Nor would anyone expect you to." Tilting her head gently. Alice studied her friend. "You say that he has lost his fortune. He was not particularly specific when he spoke with me yesterday, but stated that it was not his doing. That is why I believe he hoped you would wait for him to recover it, although I cannot quite understand how he intends to do so."

Lady Florence's lip curled.

"I did not dare call him foolish, but that is what I believe him to be. He told my father that it had been some grave mistake, that he had been tricked into losing everything - almost *everything* he possesses – and had then begged him thereafter to permit the betrothal to go ahead. There is a desperate clinging to the hope that he would somehow recover that fortune." A quiet laugh broke from her lips. "Of course, I found that more than a little ridiculous, as did my father."

"You will not wait for him then."

Lady Florence's head lifted, and her eyes glinted with a fresh fierceness that Alice had not seen in some time. It was as if, in rejecting Lord Foster, Lady Florence had now found herself quite free and that brought her a great relief.

"No, I have no intention of waiting for Lord Foster to do as he believes he can."

"Not even though he has asked you to?"

Lady Florence's shoulders lifted.

"*I* do not believe him. My father does not believe him and, if I am to be frank, I am more than little relieved to be free of him."

Something sharp kicked at Alice's heart as her friend spoke. It was as if her heart was pained on Lord Foster's behalf - his eagerness for Lady Florence had been more than apparent but, evidently, none of his interest had been returned by Lady Florence.

I always was concerned that Lady Florence did not truly care for Lord Foster. Is that not being evidenced now?

"And it also means that you are free to tie yourself to another." Lady Florence's eyes widened as she stared back at Alice. "You need to not pretend. It is quite alright. You have not been willing to tell me, and I understand that and do not hold it against you. But I believe that there is another gentleman whom you consider - perhaps one who touches your heart?" Lady Florence's eyes immediately began to fill with tears. She blinked them back rapidly, but her gaze became glassy, and Alice could do nothing other than apologize for speaking so bluntly. "Forgive me, I did not mean to upset you. I-"

"I have not been able to tell a single soul." Lady Florence's voice was broken, but she reached out to grasp Alice's hand. "My father is so very eager to make certain that I am fixed to a gentleman of his choosing that I have not even had the opportunity to *speak* to those I might consider myself. The occasions we have had to speak have been brief but every moment has been..." She closed her eyes, shaking her head. "I have tried to rid myself of my feelings for Lord Peterson, but I cannot."

"Then mayhap you will now have a chance to present him to your father through various means." Alice smiled encouragingly. "Mention his name, state that he has shown an interest in your company. Do whatever you can to present him to your father as a possible suitor, without being too overly eager. I am quite sure, my dear friend, that you have a chance here for happiness. It is clear that you have an affection for him. Does he return it?"

Lady Florence blinked rapidly, then gave her a jerky nod.

"Then I cannot help but be glad that you are free from Lord Foster. I do not think ill of him – and indeed, may even believe his story - but to see you happy would be the very best of things."

As she spoke, Alice could not help but think of Lord Foster and what she would have to say to him. It was clear that he had every intention of marrying Lady Florence if he were given the opportunity, but that was being snatched from him. Was there any way that he might be willing to consider another in Lady Florence's place? Might he consider her? The question dogged at her mind, bitterness in her mouth. If he was to be an impoverished gentleman, then her life with him could be very difficult indeed. But then again, to become a companion to a wretched aunt would be very troublesome also.

"I did not think that I should *ever* have the opportunity to consider a future with Lord Peterson," Lady Florence stated, her voice trembling. "Perhaps now I shall be offered that chance. I can only pray that my father will be willing to consider him."

"I am certain he shall." Pushing as much confidence into her voice as she could manage, Alice released Lady Florence's fingers. "I shall have to speak to Lord Foster and inform him that there is no hope. I do not criticize you for that, of course," she added quickly, seeing Lady Florence's eyes flare. "It seems very strange to me that a gentleman such as he should state that his fortune was stolen from him. Do you have any knowledge of what actually took place?"

Lady Florence nodded.

"He told my father that he had been cheated out of his fortune, that it had been taken from him when he had lost his senses."

"Lost his senses? In what way?"

"I could not say. My father did not give me the opportunity for much discussion for, to him, it was nothing more than an excuse for foolish behavior."

A little intrigued. Alice hesitated before she asked her next question. To pursue Lord Foster would mean a life of difficulty, but perhaps it was one that she could willingly face regardless, knowing what else she would face if she remained a spinster.

"I am aware that you knew him better than I. Might I ask if he was a gentleman with a penchant for gambling?"

Lady Florence shook her head.

"He certainly was not. That is why I was a little surprised at the news that he had lost his coin during a game of cards." A frown pulled lines into her forehead. "My dear Alice, you are not thinking of speaking with him of this, are you? For what purpose?"

"I have something in mind, my dear friend, but I shall not inform you of it at present. It may be the most ridiculous thing I have ever done, but under the circumstances, I believe it is for the best."

"What circumstances?" Lady Florence had moved a little closer as though she could somehow convince Alice to stop behaving in this manner. Looking her directly in the eye, she planted both hands on her hips. "You must stay away from Lord Foster. You have no poor circumstances of your own and you will certainly damage your reputation if you remain in his company."

A slightly broken laugh came from Alice's lips.

"My dear friend, my circumstances *are* this difficult, I am afraid. I have no great fortune and shall soon return home without a suitor. My father will send me away to be a companion to an aunt, and I have no wish to become such a thing. If there is any opportunity for me to change such circumstances, then I will grasp them - even if that means inclining myself towards the company of Lord Foster."

Lady Florence's eyes remained fixed on Alice's, but she was in no mood to be turned from her path.

"I did not know."

Alice shrugged.

"I had no need to tell you, not when you were soon to be betrothed – I did not want to injure your forthcoming happiness – and now when you have so much difficulty of your own."

Lady Florence swallowed.

"Then what do you intend to do?"

Her voice had gone very quiet indeed.

"I am not quite certain as yet." Speaking honestly, Alice spread her hands. "But I have in mind to make him a... a bargain, if you will. One where I might have a contented future."

"But how can you have a contented future with a gentleman who has so little fortune?" Lady Florence's brow puckered as she looked at Alice. "If you have no coin, then you cannot live a contented life. It will be one of struggle."

"Ah, but what if he does recover his fortune?" Alice smiled quickly, aware that her friend was unable to see the full machinations of her mind, and thus remained in a state of confusion. "Have no doubt that I shall take the utmost care, but I am quite determined. It is the only way I can see a brighter future for myself and, despite the risks, it is a path I am willing to take."

It took Alice some time to find Lord Foster. The ball was loud and was a crush, with so many guests it was difficult to move. She had been present for at least one hour before she finally managed to catch sight of him. He did not appear eager to join in with the rest of the revelers, for he stood to one side and continued to watch them, as she had seen him do at the previous ball. Perhaps he was afraid that news of his situation would become known to the rest of society, and she could not blame him for that fear. Now that Lord Both-well was aware of it, it was only a matter of time before he told his friends and acquaintances.

"Alice, where are you going?"

Alice glanced into the eyes of her sister. Henrietta was pouting as usual, although her eyes were a little narrowed.

"I am taking a turn around the room."

"You cannot do so. You have no chaperone."

Henrietta's voice lifted, a tiny smile tugging at her mouth. Clearly, she was eager to prevent Alice from having any enjoyment whatsoever during the evening, but Alice was not about to permit her sister to prevent her from doing so. A wry smile lifted the edge of her mouth.

"That may be the case for you, my dear sister, but our parents do not care what I do."

"You shall not find a match if you do not start behaving a little more properly." Henrietta's narrowed eyes lifted to Alice's, her lip curling. "That is why no gentleman will consider you. It is because you are entirely improper."

"That is not the case, my dear sister." Although Henrietta's words needled her, Alice chose not to rise to it. "It is because our honorable mother and esteemed father have decided to pour the entirety of their hopes into you. You are to make the very best match. *You* are to wed a gentleman of fortune, to become highly spoken of in society with a comfortable future - and I am set to become a companion to our wretched aunt living at the coast." Henrietta's eyes flickered and Alice's brows lifted. Was her sister unaware of this? She had always assumed that Henrietta had known of her mother's intentions. "That is, unless I am willing to do such things as walk around the ballroom by myself, in the hope of finding a suitable match somehow. How many gentlemen will see me otherwise?" Henrietta's lips flattened and Alice's shoulders dropped. Shaking her head, she let her voice soften a little. "Our mother and father will do nothing to aid me so therefore, I must do it myself – and I *shall* do so. Of that you can be quite sure."

Turning away swiftly, she made her way across the ballroom before Henrietta could say another word, only to come face to face with Lord Foster himself. His hand grasped hers and she did not pull it away.

"Miss Lawrence." The eagerness in his voice and the light in his eyes were unmistakable. "Pray tell me, have you spoken to Lady Florence?"

"Yes, I have." Alice did not hold back the truth, nor did she try to wrap it in sentiment and gentleness. "I am afraid you have no hope there." The building light in Lord Foster's eyes immediately faded, turning them from hazelnut brown to very dark indeed. His eyebrows drooped over them, and he lowered his head for a moment or two, pulling his gaze away. "I am sorry."

His head lifted sharply and looked directly into her face.

"It is not your doing. You have nothing to apologize for."

Hesitating, Alice twisted her hands together in front of her, in much the same way as her stomach was twisting.

"Lord Foster, you are adamant that this situation is not of your making. Is that the truth?"

His jaw tightened perceptibly, his eyes narrowing just a little.

"Yes, it is true." Hard edges tipped his words. "It is a ridiculous thing to believe. I quite understand that, but still..." Lifting his shoulders, he held them there for a moment and then dropped them. "I had hoped that Lady Florence would think more of me."

"Yes, I understand," Alice spoke as gently as she could, ignoring the pounding of her heart. "I have something of a proposition for you." He looked startled, and she hurried on before she could lose her courage. "I shall aid you in this search to recover your fortune. I shall be an ally to you in society, and will speak well of you to others. I promise to tell my companions and my friends and my acquaintances that your loss of fortune is not of your own doing. In short, Lord Foster, I will be your ally. I will do whatever I can to aid you, but for a price."

Lord Foster's eyebrows lifted.

"And what price would that be?"

The knot which had tied itself in Alice's stomach now turned into fluttering butterflies. She took a moment to regain her composure, steadying herself before she spoke again.

"You shall marry me."

To her horror, Lord Foster immediately chuckled. The face which had held lines of grief only a few moments ago was now wreathed in smiles.

"You are a most forward young lady." Shaking his head in either admiration or mockery, he continued to grin. "I do not know you well, but I am quite determined to find my own bride when the right time comes. I may not be able to wed Lady Florence, but I am certain that..."

"What are you so certain of?" Speaking harshly, her face burning, Alice spread both hands. "Do you fully expect to be able to return to society when news of your poverty echoes through London? That there will be young ladies eager to be in your company?"

Shaking her head, she held his gaze for a long moment, then turned sharply and walked away, her head held high.

Anger filled her as she made her way back to her mother, embarrassment burning hot through her veins. She had not expected him to laugh and yet his supposed belief that all should be quite well in society with regard to his standing was quite laughable! Daring a glance over her shoulder to where she had left Lord Foster, she saw, to her surprise, that he was standing in the same position as she had left him, staring after her as though he had somehow been caught in a trance. Her eyebrows lifted as their gazes met, but Lord Foster quickly looked away. Alice could not tell what he was thinking, but at the very least, there was no laughter in his face any longer - but that did not mean he thought any more of her suggestion. The only thing she could do at present was to wait and see.

CHAPTER FIVE

"*T*hank you for coming with me this afternoon."

"But of course." Lord Wiltsham gave him a brief smile before returning his attention to the door which blocked them from Lord Gillespie's house. "I have as much eagerness to find out the truth from Lord Gillespie as you. It is strange that he has been absent from society these last few days."

"I quite agree, which is why I am all the more grateful to him for being willing to allow us to call upon him this afternoon."

Rapping again a little more sharply, William let out a frustrated sigh. The butler was taking some time to answer the door.

"Some of my staff removed themselves from my house this afternoon." Lord Wiltsham sighed heavily. "I was able to find them new employment. I am glad of that at least."

William nodded, his jaw tightening.

"I have instructed my man of business to put my greys up for sale." Keeping his voice low, he did not look at his friend, frustrated with the mixture of anger and pain that shot through him. "I have no other recourse. I had thought - foolishly, perhaps - that I would be able to recover my fortune easily. But I am slowly beginning to realize that it is much more complex than I first imagined."

"I returned to that place." Lord Wiltsham shot William a glance. "It may have been unwise of me, but I wanted to see if I could meet with anyone who had been there that night."

William looked over at him.

"And were you successful?"

Lord Wiltsham shook his head.

"It was claimed that I had never set foot in that establishment before. My anger became so great that I had to step away and the door was closed so firmly behind me that I do not think I would ever be permitted again to enter."

"I am sorry for that. But you were wise to go and seek out answers in the very place you lost your fortune."

Why have I never thought of doing such a thing?

"Lord Gillespie does not appear to be at home. Either that or his butler is so slow and deaf that he has not heard our knocking!" Changing the subject, Lord Wiltsham knocked again, for what was the third time, on the heavy door. "You are certain that this was the correct time for us to call?"

"Yes, I am quite certain."

His frustration getting the better of him. William put out one hand and turned the door handle and, much to his surprise, it opened without any difficulty. There was nothing locking it from the inside, then.

"Whatever are you doing?" Lord Wiltsham hissed, putting out one hand to hold William back. "We cannot simply walk into another gentleman's house!"

"But we have been invited," William reminded him.

"Given that he was the one who sent us to that particular place in London where we all lost our fortunes, I have no intention of being left standing on his doorstep. He ought not to hide!" His frustration still pushing him forward, William stepped into the house and looked around. It was a little dim but, given that there was no bright sunshine today, that was to be expected. No servants moved around the house, and neither did the butler appear, despite the fact that William lifted his voice and called for him. His words echoed around the seemingly empty house and William's stomach twisted. "Something is wrong."

Lord Wiltsham snorted.

"There is nothing wrong. Lord Gillespie clearly does not wish to speak to us and has decided to pretend he is not at home. Perhaps, he has left the house entirely, to avoid us!"

"But that does not explain why there are no servants." William took some steps forward, his footsteps echoing on the floor. "Nor does it explain why we received a note from him encouraging us to call today. Why would he send such a note if he was not expecting us to arrive?"

Lord Wiltsham threw up his hands.

"I do not know, but all the same, I feel most uncomfortable walking into another gentlemen's house without his permission. I think we should simply return home and write to Lord Gillespie again thereafter. Our reputations are damaged enough already. We do not want to make anything worse."

William shook his head.

"If you wish to take your leave, I shall not hold it against you. For myself, I am determined to find Lord Gillespie, wherever he is hiding, and demand the answers that I have requested."

It was as though Lord Gillespie held William's future tightly in his hands. Either William could leave him to cling onto it, to hide any brightness from the rest of his life, or he could find him and demand that it be released from his grip. Making his way forward into the house, he marched swiftly across the hallway and down towards Lord Gillespie's drawing room and study. He had been in this house before, but the memory of which room was which was lost to him. He tried one room and then the next, walking through the parlor, the library, and the drawing room until he came to what he assumed was Lord Gillespie's study.

"It is very strange, I grant you, that there is no one else present in the house."

William's skin prickled as Lord Wiltsham's voice echoed behind him. Turning, he lifted one eyebrow.

"You decided to remain then."

Lord Wiltsham said nothing, leaving William to turn the handle of the study door and step inside.

As soon as he did, everything changed in an instant, for Lord Gillespie was present, certainly, but from the way he was slumped across the desk, William realized that he was almost certainly dead.

"Whatever is the matter?" Stepping in behind William, Lord Wiltsham let out a gasp of horror. "Good gracious! Do you think he is...?"

"Given that his eyes are open, but he is not moving, I would say that yes, Lord Gillespie is no longer of this world."

William's shock caused his heart to beat painfully fast. Blood was roaring in his ears, and he could not lift his hand from the door handle.

"We should leave." Lord Wiltsham's hand grasped William's arm. "Come, we *must* depart."

William did not move, despite his friend's insistent hand. He stared at the slumped figure of Lord Gillespie, devastation filling his mind. Lord Gillespie was dead. Then he could tell them nothing about why he had sent them to the gambling houses in the east end of London. He could give them no explanation, could not tell them whether or not he had been involved in the scheme.

"Come." Lord Wiltsham's fingers tightened, and William was pulled bodily backward. "We must leave at once!"

It still took William some moments to respond, but eventually, he allowed Lord Wiltsham to walk him out of Lord Gillespie's study. The two gentlemen stared at each other as they stood in the silent hallway, joined in their rapid breathing from the shock. Pins and needles were making their way through William's limbs, bringing a coldness behind them that seemed to take over every part of his being.

"Lord Gillespie is dead."

Speaking those words aloud seemed to make it even worse. Staring at Lord Wiltsham, William tried to consider what he ought to do next, but nothing came to his mind. It remained dull, frozen in shock at the horrific discovery they had made.

A sudden sound behind them made both gentlemen whirl around. The next second, William found his legs moving quickly towards the front door. He did not know who else was in the house, but he certainly did not want to be caught standing next to the room where Lord Gillespie lay dead. Lord Wiltsham hurried with him, and together they stepped outside, closing the door slowly behind them. It did not make much of a sound save for a single creak, although that in itself was enough to make William wince.

"What shall we do?"

William stared into Lord Wiltsham's pale face. His friend was looking for him to come up with some sort of plan, but William's mind remained entirely blank.

"My Lords, I did wonder if I heard someone knocking. You must forgive me. Lord Gillespie sent us all below stairs for a short while."

It took William a few moments to realize that the door was now open, and that Lord Gillespie's butler was standing in the doorway.

"Yes... thank you." Hearing the rough croak in his voice, he cleared his throat and clasped his hands behind his back. "Is Lord Gillespie at home? We had a note from him inviting us to call at this time."

Giving the butler their names, they stepped inside after him. The man disappeared, leaving William and Lord Wiltsham to stand silently together, their hands clasped lightly in front of them. It was very strange to be waiting for a gentleman that they both knew would never appear.

"I do not know if we are even doing the right thing." William threw a glance towards Lord Wiltsham, who merely shrugged, his face rather white. "What if we should-"

A scream followed by a loud exclamation of voices soon followed. Evidently, Lord Gillespie had been found.

~

"Gentlemen." A man came to stand directly in front of them as they tried to enter White's. "Lord Wiltsham and Lord Foster, is it not?"

"Yes." William, in desperate need of a brandy, folded

his arms tight across his chest. "Is there a reason that you are blocking our path? We are patrons here."

"I am afraid you cannot be so any longer." The man gave them a tight smile, speaking with authority. "News of your current financial situation has reached us and as such, we are no longer able to continue with your membership of White's at present. That is, unless you have the funds to not only clear your tab, but also to pay for your continued membership."

William flicked a glance towards Lord Wiltsham. The gentleman was still white-faced, although his eyes now began to blaze with the fire which had also ignited itself in William's stomach.

"You will let us into White's." Lord Wiltsham stepped forward, one hand pointing towards the man's chest. "I am aware of the betting book within White's, but I did not think that you would be someone who would take such rumors so seriously. For that is all they are. They are *only* rumors."

The man did not appear to believe them.

"Be that as it may," he replied, lifting his chin as his gaze became steely. "You are not permitted to enter unless you can do as I have asked."

The hardness in his tone made William wince and he turned his head away. All he wanted to do was to sit in White's and forget about Lord Gillespie as he sipped a large glass of the finest brandy. He had always enjoyed a brandy at White's, ever since his first days in London.

Now it seemed that pleasure was to be taken from him.

"Come, Wiltsham. Let us go and find another establishment... one which is not so persnickety."

Throwing a hard look at the broad-shouldered man, William turned away from him, ignoring the fact that his heart was dragging lower with every step. Not stopping to check whether or not Lord Wiltsham was following him, William strode away. Anger was bubbling near the surface, but he did not permit it to express itself anywhere other than in his heart. He had known this was coming. He had tried to ignore it, but it had been impossible to avoid. News of his poverty had reached the echelons of society, and now he was doomed in their eyes.

Perhaps it does not matter whether or not I will ever regain my fortune. To them, it matters only that I have lost it.

It was painful to realize that he might never again achieve the status he had once held in society.

At once, the words of Miss Lawrence came back to him. He had laughed at her suggestion, believing his future was not as bleak as she had stated, and quite certain that he would not require the services of a young woman to aid him in regaining his fortune. But now that he had been ejected from White's, he began to wonder whether or not Miss Lawrence's proposal ought to be taken up. After all, it did not appear as though he would ever be able to find a wife - not for many years, at least, and that was not something he wished to delay. He wanted to enjoy time with his wife, wanted to raise a family. The truth of it was that society could continue to reject him, even if he regained his fortune. The scandal could linger for many years, meaning he might well be in his dotage before he was able to secure a bride, and even then, there was no guarantee that she would be a lady of quality. He might have to settle for the daughter of a Baronet!

And here now is the opportunity to wed the daughter of a Viscount.

"You are troubled." Lord Wiltsham's voice was hard. "I

confess that anger is my strongest emotion, however. I did not think we would be ejected so soon from White's."

"It seems that Lord Bothwell has not kept my revelation to him a secret." William shook his head. "And no doubt many of our servants were of aid to this also, whispering to each other that you have had to find many of your staff new employment."

"It is altogether unpleasant. I know that I and the other gentleman are doing as much as we can. But with Lord Gillespie dead, it feels as though we are at the end already, before we have even begun. He can tell us nothing. We have come up empty." William turned just in time to see Lord Wiltsham passing one hand over his eyes. "Perhaps there is naught for us to do but to accept our fate."

"I shall not permit myself to think so." Stopping, William put one hand on his friend's shoulder. "Do not give in to despair. We shall find a way yet." Lord Wiltsham shook his head, but did not verbally disagree. "We shall. I am *sure* we shall."

"I think I must return to my seat for a short while." Lord Wiltsham shrugged. "In light of my predicament, I must look at my finances. I have been delaying it but, given the situation with Lord Gillespie, I can do so no longer."

William wanted to beg him to stay, so that they might fight on together, otherwise he would be entirely alone in London.

"I will return soon." Lord Wiltsham smiled briefly, although his eyes remained heavy. "I am aware that the other gentlemen are also gone to their estates, but I fear I must join them - but one of us shall return to be with you soon." His eyes darted upwards towards William's face, then dropped away again. "That is, unless you also intend to return to your estate."

William shook his head.

"No, I cannot. I have lost both my fortune, Lady Florence, and now my reputation. To return to my estate would be akin to accepting defeat. My spirits would not permit me to do so."

"Noted. I am sorry that Lady Florence will not wait for you to regain your reputation and your fortune."

"It was foolish of me to expect otherwise." William grimaced, then shook his head. "Her friend, Miss Lawrence, has offered me something. Initially I thought it the most ridiculous notion in all of England's history, but now that I have come to think of it a little more, I begin to wonder whether or not it may be wise." They began to walk again, although the silence was filled with Lord Wiltsham's unspoken questions. William obliged him with an answer. "She has offered to aid me in my struggle."

"Indeed? But she knows nothing of the specifics as yet surely?"

"She does not, but she seeks to help my reputation in society so that I do not lose it entirely. I will admit that I have very little certainty as to how much influence a Viscount's daughter can have on society, but she is willing and I do not think, at this point, that I can sensibly refuse. I need any help that is offered!"

"That is very good of the lady. She has a kindness in her, I think."

William coughed, knowing that further explanation was needed.

"I am not able to say whether or not the lady has a kind heart. I have told you that she will aid me in whatever way she can - but only if I wed her, once I have reclaimed my fortune."

Lord Wiltsham stopped dead. Despite his own many

tumultuous thoughts, William could not help but laugh at the sheer astonishment which had appeared on his friend's face.

"And... and you are considering this?" Spluttering, Lord Wiltsham made his feelings known as he threw up his hands. "That is –"

"I confess that at first, I thought it more than a little ridiculous. I laughed at the lady and saw her eyes flush with such an anger that I quickly realized she was being entirely sincere. That was only yesterday, I confess, and I then took to considering the matter a little more. It has only been now, now that I have been thrown from White's, that I realize the true difficulties of my present circumstances. Therefore, I begin to wonder if it might not be a sensible idea."

"You cannot be serious. You are saying such a thing only to lift my spirits."

Lord Wiltsham crossed his arms over his chest and glared, narrow-eyed, at William.

"I must confess the truth. I am speaking to you honestly." William's smile shattered as he explained his reasoning. "I shall have no good reputation in society, regardless of whether or not I regain my fortune. There will always be whispers and rumors about how I came to lose it in the first place, and perhaps even more about how I regained it thereafter. It may be a great many years before I can even consider finding a wife and, even then, I may struggle to find a suitable lady eager to wed me." Spreading his hands, he shrugged. "The daughter of a Viscount, who is young and of decent character, does not seem to be an entirely displeasing suggestion and the truth is, I fear that I may never be able to marry at all if I do not take this chance! I cannot see whether or not she will be of any real use to me in my present difficulties, but her offer of help is the only one I have."

"Then you will accept her. Even though you have very little knowledge of her character or her family."

"Yes, I believe I shall."

Such confirmation, even to himself, made him fear he was being a little unwise, but William nodded to himself, determination growing.

"Have you ever asked yourself what reason she has for suggesting such a thing, and why she is yet unwed? Perhaps there are hidden significant defects in her character, which prevent any gentleman from considering her. Besides which, she is not particularly handsome!"

Lord Wiltsham lifted one eyebrow as William shook his head.

"I confess I have not considered that, but that does not mean that I will immediately refuse her, based on that fear. I will speak to her again at length, and if I am satisfied with everything that she tells me, then I fully expect to begin courting the young lady very soon, with the full intention of marrying her... once my fortune is restored."

Lord Wiltsham lifted an eyebrow.

"And if it is never restored?"

William frowned, a line forming between his eyebrows. He had not thought particularly in depth about any of the details, but he was not to be deterred.

"Then I suspect I shall marry her regardless, so long as she is contented to marry a pauper," he replied a little brusquely. "As I have said, I have not spoken to her at length, but I shall do so. It is the only course I have available to take."

CHAPTER SIX

"*I* hear Henrietta has done very well."

Alice immediately dropped her gaze to the table, refusing to look at either her sister or her parents. She had no wish to hear her father simpering over his youngest daughter when she was so clearly a disappointment despite doing nothing to deserve such displeasure.

"Yes, Henrietta has done very well. There are many gentlemen eager for her company. I am certain that you will have many gentlemen callers, although it is a shame that we are to be out this afternoon."

"Where are we to go, mama?"

Having not heard of any intention to take themselves out of the house, Alice looked inquiringly towards her mother, whose gaze was still focused on her youngest. Lady Blackford waved around one hand in her direction as though her question was irritating.

"Henrietta requires a new pair of gloves and a new bonnet. We are all to take ourselves into town for a short while. You will accompany us, of course."

There would be no new gloves for Alice, of course. This

did not come as a surprise to her, although her disappointment rose into a growing frustration that took over every part of her. Her fingers curled into fists under the table, and she dropped her gaze to her hands once more so that she would not permit any frustration to escape into her expression. Henrietta was the chosen child. Beautiful, where Alice was not, her character was slowly becoming spoiled and selfish. Not that such a thing mattered to their mother, however, for she was only interested in just how good a match Henrietta could make, so that she might boast of it to her acquaintances and revel in the wealth and status that her new son-in-law would bring.

Alice did not matter at all.

She would trail after her mother and sister this afternoon, looking at all the beautiful things, but being permitted to purchase none, given she did not even have any pin money of her own - but Henrietta would be given more than enough to satisfy any whim.

"And Henrietta, you shall wear your new gloves to this evening's soiree." Lady Blackford's words were sickly sweet. "I am certain you will draw the attention of even *more* gentlemen." She laughed brightly. "You will have your pick of suitors."

Looking away quickly so that her mother did not catch the grimace which pulled at her expression, Alice let out a surreptitious sigh. There would be no suitors for her. Her only hope had been Lord Foster, but he had turned down her offer of an alliance by laughing in her face. The only gratification she had resulted from an awareness that he would not be able to spread what she had done into society, given that he was so disregarded already. However, she did not regret asking him, and if she should come face to face with him again, she would not drop her gaze with embarrassment. No, he would see that *he* was the one who had made the mistake, not her. It might take a little time, but Alice was certain that he would come to regret turning down her offer of aid.

A gentle rap at the door indicated that one of the servants wished to enter, and Lord Blackford called them forth. Alice gave them very little attention as the footman came in with a note in his hand. She was entirely astonished, however, when the note was subsequently delivered to her. The whole room fell silent. Alice did not very often receive notes, for there were no gentlemen to call on her, no one to write her sonnets. Occasionally, she might hear from Lady Florence, but given that they were in each other's company on an almost daily basis, there was very little need for notes to be written between them.

"Alice." Her mother arched one eyebrow. "Who has been writing to you?"

Opening up the note quickly, Alice glanced at it and instantly the astonishment caught tight in her chest.

Lord Foster.

"It is no one of importance, Mama." Folding the note up quickly without even reading it, she slipped it into her pockets and smiled. "It is only Lady Florence. She is in deep despair." Her smile faded as she quickly came up with an excuse. "I am sure that you have heard that the gentleman who courted her has lost his fortune, and therefore, their courtship has come to an end."

This served as an excellent distraction from the note she had received, and soon her mother and Henrietta were busy discussing Lady Florence's beauty, her gowns, and her canceled betrothal. Alice slipped away from the table before they even had a chance to notice she was gone, hurrying up to her room and closing the door tightly behind her.

Turning the note over in her hand, she took a moment before she opened it. What would be his reasons for writing? To apologize to her for his laughter? Was it to thank her for her offer, but to kindly refuse again? Could it possibly be that he had changed his mind?

Letting out a slow breath, Alice closed her eyes, then turned to the letter. Unfolding it, she read it quickly. The letter was short, but his hand was neat, his meaning quite clear after only the first line.

'Miss Lawrence.

After some deliberation, I should like to speak to you again about the matter we discussed previously. I have some questions, but I am of a mind to accept you, should the answers to my questions be acceptable. I shall be at the ball this evening, although keeping back from the crowd, given my status in society at present. Indeed, I am grateful that my invitation to the ball itself has not been rescinded! Perhaps you might seek me out so that we can discuss the matter together.'

Alice did not keep the note for long. Reading it over once more, she quickly ripped it into small pieces and then buried it into the coals of the as yet unlit fire. It would be burnt up when the maid laid the fire the following morning. Her mother was often a devious creature, and Alice did not want her to read the letter which Lord Foster had sent. The situation and her plan were entirely her own, and Alice did not require her mother's input or permission.

A small smile spread across her face. Now, at least there was hope. It might not be a fiery hope, but it was hope, nonetheless. Hope that she could have a future with a husband, and perhaps even a family of her own. A hope that she would no longer be looked at as someone only fit to be a companion and, instead, might have the chance of a life of her own. It was certainly not the most common way to achieve such a desire, but it was the only option available to her. She could only pray now that whatever questions Lord Foster had for her, she would be able to answer them in a way that he would find satisfactory - for then, her future might hold a brilliant brightness instead of dull and shadowy clouds.

~

"YOU HAVE FOUND ME."

"Yes, Lord Foster, it would appear so."

Alice, who again was not missed at all by her mother and sister, had made her way slowly around the room, not looked at by any gentleman or lady. Her eyes had lingered on almost every gentleman, but it was not until she reached the French doors that she finally spotted her quarry.

"You received my note."

Alice studied him for a moment. There were dark shadows under his eyes and no smile on his lips. He appeared to be brooding, but she could not blame him for that, given the circumstances. Everyone here would be talking of him - no doubt further invitations would be rescinded, and he would have less and less opportunity to appear in society. The *ton* would not tolerate a gentleman who had lost his fortune in a foolish game of gambling. Almost everyone knew of it now.

"I believe I am here this evening so that our host may gain a little more interest in his event." Lord Foster's eyes flickered, and his smile was angry. "I am a good talking point, it seems."

"I am sorry for that. Regardless of what you have done, there is no need for the *ton* to treat you in such a way."

Immediately, Lord Foster's brows drew together so quickly that she half expected a thunderclap.

"Let me make one thing very plain to you." Lord Foster took a step closer, and Alice held both hands around her waist in a protective gesture. He seemed suddenly intimidating, brooding, and dark. "This... this agreement or bargain or whatever it is we shall call it, can only go ahead if you believe that I am telling the truth. I did not lose my fortune through deliberate actions. That is why I am so very frustrated. It is not right that I should be treated as though I was *intentionally* selfish or foolish when I have done nothing wrong. If you cannot believe that. Miss Lawrence, then there is nothing for us to discuss. The matter is over."

Licking her lips, Alice had dropped her gaze for a moment, then lifted it again. Lord Foster was being entirely reasonable, she considered, although she did find his manner a little intimidating.

"I quite understand, Lord Foster. You shall, however, have to explain it to me in its entirety before I can come to any sort of conclusion."

Lord Foster scowled, and his brows dropped low over his eyes, but he did not refuse.

"Very well. But before I do so, might we consider the situation before us? If you believe me, and if I accept what you have suggested, then what happens if I do not recover my fortune?" One eyebrow arched. "You may find yourself in a situation where you must marry a pauper. Have you considered that?"

Alice nodded.

"I have and I am willing to accept it. It is not a life that anyone should want, but it is one that I will take on."

Lord Foster's brow lifted suddenly. He looked back at

her with those dark eyes, flickering questions held within the orbs.

"One might wonder why a lady of quality would be willing to do such a thing."

His voice was low and quiet, and yet a deep flush began to rise in her chest, spreading heat up into her neck and her cheeks.

"If you are suggesting that I have something to hide from you, something that a quick marriage will fix, then you are entirely mistaken." Speaking with as much dignity as she could, she lifted her chin and gazed at him steadily. "If I can be entirely truthful, it is because I have no better option. Soon my father will send me to my aunt, who lives far from here, to be a companion. I shall be her drudge. I fully expect that, should that come to pass, I will never see my father, sister, nor mother again."

Instead of appearing surprised, Lord Foster only frowned again.

"I find that all the more astonishing. Why would a gentleman push his eligible elder daughter away from society?"

"Because his eldest daughter is not particularly handsome." Her face was still burning, but Alice did not hold the truth back. "I have not the beauty of face that my younger sister does. My mother sees nothing but fault and failure with me, but evidently sees naught but beauty and promise in Henrietta. *She* will gain a good husband, good standing, and a fortune, whereas I will not even be allowed to seek such a thing. My parents' efforts go to her rather than to me. They would be glad to be rid of me, which I believe is their sole intention."

Lord Foster studied her, his gaze going to her face as if deciding whether or not such considerations were justified.

Alice looked back at him but did not allow her gaze to flinch. Heat continued to rise in her face, but she ignored it, refusing to permit such a look to cow her.

"Therefore, I would be saving you as much as you would be saving me."

Alice allowed herself a gentle shrug at his remark.

"I believe, Lord Foster, that you may end up aiding me *more* than I can aid you. What happens if you cannot regain your fortune? I will do all that I can to help you, but there is no assurance that you will be successful. Whereas I, it seems, can rely on you to take me as your bride when the time is right."

His dark eyes flashed away for a moment and then returned to her. His jaw was tight as if he were biting his cheek hard on the inside as he considered his decision. Alice looked back at him steadily, waiting for him to give a response that would either seal her fate or decide her future.

"Very well." Her heart sped in shock and her throat closed up. "We have an agreement. You will aid me in recovering my fortune, to the best of your ability, and in regaining my status in society. And I shall take you as my bride. What will your father say to that?"

This was not something that Alice had ever considered.

"I cannot say for certain, but I do not think that he can refuse me. After all, his words to me were that I must find a suitor for myself by the end of the Season. Otherwise, I should become a companion." A wry smile tipped her mouth. "I do not think that he believed I should have any success, however."

"Then let us hope that he does not find fault with our match." Lord Foster's face flushed with a sudden heat, as though he had only just realized what he had agreed to. "I must ask you again, Miss Lawrence, whether or not you believe that what I have told you is the truth. I do not think that our arrangement can go ahead unless you do so."

"I believe that there is a question over how you lost your fortune." Speaking honestly, Alice found herself unwilling to lie, despite the consequences of doing so. "As I have said, you will have to tell me all. When can such a thing be arranged?"

Lord Foster blinked.

"Tomorrow? Perhaps we shall consider it our first outing together. Might you consider a walk with me in Hyde Park?"

Something swirled in Alice's stomach, but she dismissed it quickly. The last thing she needed to do was to begin to have feelings for Lord Foster. This was naught but a practical and suitable arrangement. There was no need for emotion.

"Will you be there during the fashionable hour? I believe my mother and sister intend to be present tomorrow, and of course, I must attend with them. They will not notice if I depart with you for a short while, nor will they care."

Speaking off-handedly, she did not see the flash of surprise in Lord Foster's expression. However, she did notice the way that his eyes rounded a little, and the way he tilted his head to one side. Did he have sympathy for her? Or was he only surprised at her lack of propriety?

"Tomorrow, at the fashionable hour would suit me very well. We shall take a walk together and I will tell you everything, including something which has only recently occurred, for it is just as relevant as the rest, I think."

The urge to ask him what this was rose in Alice, but she did not allow it to be spoken.

"Very well. Tomorrow, during the fashionable hour."

She bobbed a curtsey, looking back into the eyes of the

gentleman who, one day soon, would become her husband. Should all go well, she would stand up beside him in church and make her promises, and soon after become mistress of his house.

If there is any house to be mistress of!

"Thank you, Lord Foster. I look forward to seeing you tomorrow."

Lord Foster nodded. His eyes were already back across the room, looking away from her, as though now that their arrangements had been made, he had no need to further this conversation.

"Tomorrow, Miss Lawrence. Good evening to you."

A little surprised at the swift sting of pain which entered her heart. Alice lifted her lips in a smile and ignored everything else. She was not about to become emotional over Lord Foster. Their arrangement was made, and the discussion was over, so of course, it was natural that he did not need to pay her any further attention. Turning on her heel, she made her way back toward her sister and her mother. Neither of them noticed her reappearance. Henrietta was too busy talking to three gentlemen who were all studying her in rapt amazement, as though every word she spoke was prophetic, and Lady Blackford looked on, pride in her broad smile and twinkling eyes.

It was an expression that Alice would never be able to place on her mother's face, no matter what she did.

But now, at least, I shall not be alone for the rest of my days. I shall not be a drudge. I will not be under the thumb of my father's rule and forced to become a companion to an old aunt until I too am of an age where I require a companion.

A small smile pulled at her lips.

I am to be Lady Foster.

CHAPTER SEVEN

*W*illiam shook his head to himself. He had received a note from Lord Wiltsham only a few moments ago telling him that the fellow had returned to his estate and did not know when he would be back in London. It was obvious that Lord Wiltsham was heavy-hearted over the situation and struggling to come to terms with his new state, and William could not blame him for that. It was indeed a dreadful situation. Having already been ejected from White's, he had received not one, but two notes, telling him that previous invitations were now rescinded - and he fully expected that more would come. To those who still extended an invitation to him, it would be for their own benefit as his presence would, no doubt, garner the interest of those in society who reveled in others' misery.

But I shall not return to my estate. Slamming one fist on the table, William shook his head again, then glanced at the clock. He only had a few minutes before he needed to prepare for his walk with Miss Lawrence.

Miss Lawrence, who is to be my bride.

The shock of such a thought ran straight through him

and he gripped his quill hard to the point that it bent and then snapped completely. All the more irritated, William slammed his fist down hard on the desk again, making the ink bottle rattle.

"I am becoming much too caught up with Miss Lawrence."

Speaking aloud, William dropped his broken quill, and then reached to ring the bell for his butler. He had only a sennight left before he would have to let some of his servants find other employment, but for the moment he was determined to keep them on. It gave him a small sense of security, knowing that the servants had nothing to whisper about as regarded their security in his London home as yet - but it was a security that he would soon have to break.

And all because I followed Lord Gillespie's advice.

Shaking his head to himself, William pushed fingers through his disordered hair and then stood up abruptly from his desk.

It had been one moment. One moment when he had chosen to do as an acquaintance suggested, and thereafter had come nothing but problems. Had Lord Gillespie known that William and the rest of his friends would go into the gaming hell and lose their fortunes? Had he felt any guilt over the matter? There were so many unanswered questions that lingered, burning through William's mind as he began to pace around the room, trying not to allow anger to take hold of him.

It feels as though my life is spinning out of control.

He had been perfectly contented before. A gentleman in London, who had finally found himself a bride. Lady Florence had been beautiful, her character gentle, and she was everything that he believed he needed in a wife. Now, however, he had lost her, as well as his fortune. His reputation was sinking slowly and the only person who seemed able to be of any aid to him was Miss Lawrence. She had promised that she believed his loss of fortune had not been his doing, but whether or not she truly, in her heart of hearts, believed that he spoke the truth, William did not know. To his surprise, his eagerness for her to believe his every word was growing steadily. This afternoon, he would tell her all, and a part of him ached over the thought that she might doubt him, once his explanation was finished. How much he wanted her to believe him! She was, he realized, his only ally.

I am lost.

The feeling of being entirely rudderless, drifting along without any guidance as to where one might fall, was a little overwhelming. Panic gripped his heart and William fought against it with all of his might, dropping his head and standing quite still so that he could draw in long breaths to calm himself. Despite his determination to win against this set of circumstances, concern that he could lose everything and continue to be without it for the rest of his days began to push its way deep into his mind. With Lord Gillespie dead, there was every chance that he would remain as he was at present - for where was he to turn next? He might never find out who had manipulated him in such a disastrous way. There was a chance that he could remain in poverty and, thereafter, have a wife to concern himself with also. A wife would be another mouth to feed, another body to clothe. Doubts reared their head, forcing William's heart to beat with great fury and fright. Had he really been wise in accepting Miss Lawrence's bargain?

For a moment, his future drew itself out in front of him, threatening him with great and overwhelming darkness. He saw his house in London being sold, given to another who could well afford it. He saw himself in his estate, sitting by a meager fire, with only a hard bit of bread in one hand and a glass of water in the other as he shivered from the cold. The estate was crumbling, with no money to put into its improvements, and he had no one else around him. No servants, no friends, no society to speak of. Was that the future he was now looking at? Would he be the one in his family to leave a legacy of death and destruction rather than security and prosperity?

His breathing became shallow, and William froze, his eyes closed tightly and his jaw working hard. His determination was slowly receding, and his confidence was battered by these thoughts. It was foolish for him to even consider meeting with Miss Lawrence this afternoon. Perhaps this whole thing had been a dreadful mistake, and he would now find himself in a position where he would need to break what had already been agreed upon. Miss Lawrence would never forgive him, but might it be for the best?

A rap on the door broke through his musings and William shoved one hand after the other through his hair before he called for the servant to enter. The footman walked into the room without a word, bowing as he handed William a note. Murmuring his thanks, William took it from him and then waited until the fellow had left the room before he began to open it. Breaking the seal, he pulled it open eagerly, wondering if it was from Lord Wiltsham, hoping beyond hope that something had come to light that would be of help to them all.

It was not. It was from Miss Lawrence.

Lord Foster.

I thought to write to thank you for the arrangement we have made. I am aware that I may have appeared a little forthright and cannot even be certain whether or not I offered you my thanks, but I wish now to make certain that you are aware of my gratitude. I am truly grateful to you for your agreement. Even though our coming together is nothing more than practical, I can assure you that it is a great comfort to know I shall no longer be facing life as a companion. I am well aware that our future together may be difficult, but I am more than willing to stand by your side. I look forward to meeting you this afternoon so that you may tell me of the circumstances which have brought you to this difficult place. Have my assurance, Lord Foster, that I will listen carefully to you. I am ready to listen, to hear, and to understand.

The note itself was simple, but the effect it had on William's heart was significant. The panic which had filled him slowly faded away as he read over the letter one more time. It was a brief note, but he was grateful to her for her consideration in writing to him. At last, hope slowly began to rebuild itself and the fear which had surrounded him began to fade. He was not alone in this situation, and it would be foolish to push Miss Lawrence away. She was there, and she was willing to be present alongside him, in whatever happened next. Finally, he had someone willing to listen to everything he had to say, and who eagerly wanted to trust his every word. Taking in yet another long breath, William folded up the note and clutched it tightly in one hand. Miss Lawrence was quite right. Certainly, he had been a little surprised at her determination to move forward with such an arrangement, given that she might find herself struck with poverty for the rest of her days, but at the same time, William had to admit to himself that he appreciated such willingness. He could only pray that her character would turn out to be just as he hoped: one of determination, of kindness, of a willingness to listen, and of a devotion that might reach out and touch his heart. There were hints of that in her already, and that realization lifted William's heart still further.

A little surprised that the note from Miss Lawrence had affected him so greatly, William glanced down at it and then returned to his study desk. Sitting down, he considered whether or not he ought to reply but then chose not to do so, for he could express his gratitude to her for what she had written when they met.

"I am not alone in this." Speaking aloud, William slammed one hand down heavily onto his desk to emphasize his words. "I am *not* alone."

The words give him confidence, and he gazed fixedly at the door as though he expected Miss Lawrence to walk through it at any moment. Now, strangely, he could hardly wait for the fashionable hour to come, so that he might be in company with her once more.

I DO NOT THINK *her so very plain.*

A little startled at the thought that dug itself into his mind, William pulled his eyes away from the approaching figure of Miss Lawrence and looked at the ground instead. From what had been a brief glance, he had seen Miss Lawrence's grey dress billowing gently in the wind and knew immediately that it would match her eyes. That thought had been a pleasing one, although he had found himself immediately struck with surprise that he should think such a thing and, indeed, would find pleasure in that thought... hence why his eyes were now fixed to the ground.

"Good afternoon."

"Good afternoon, Miss Lawrence."

Unable to keep his eyes on the ground anymore.

William looked up and found his heart jolting in a very strange manner. Miss Lawrence smiled, and he saw that he had been quite right to assume that color of her dress would match her eyes. It drew his attention to them, emphasizing them and making them seem almost silver in appearance. Why he should find himself so captivated by her eyes brought William nothing but confusion, however, and he gave himself a small shake, refusing to acknowledge the unexpected, swirling emotions that coursed through him now.

"Are you quite all right, Lord Foster?"

"Yes, of course." Clearing his throat, he turned away from the gathering crowd in Hyde Park. "I would suggest we take a short stroll, but if your mother and sister—"

"My mother and sister will not even notice that I am gone."

There was a nonchalance in her voice that did not match the darkening of her grey eyes. They grew a little heavier, like clouds filled with rain, and a spark of sympathy shot through William's core.

"Then perhaps we should walk in sight of the crowd, but not close to it," he suggested, offering her his arm. "It is not yet as busy as it will be, but it will be crowded enough, I am sure."

"Yes, I quite agree." With a small smile, Miss Lawrence accepted his arm, and they began to walk slowly together along the path. The sounds of birdsong clashed with the laughter and conversation which came from the gathering crowd of ladies and gentlemen - who of course had come to see others as well as to be seen themselves. "I believe you were to tell me about what happened that night, Lord Foster." Miss Lawrence glanced up at him, her smile soft. "I know that you must have a great eagerness to tell me of it and we need not indulge in any other conversation. Please, begin."

Relief flooded him as he smiled back at her, grateful that she saw just how important this was to him.

"Thank you, Miss Lawrence." Taking in a deep breath, and ignoring the swell that rose in his heart, he began to talk, telling Miss Lawrence exactly what had happened. "I woke up the following morning to find myself quite confused," he finished. "I can assure you, Miss Lawrence, that I am not the sort of gentleman who would *ever* give away my fortune. I would never be foolish enough to take that sort of bet, where so much was at stake. I may be foolish in many things, but I am not foolish when it comes to my responsibilities to the title. Lady Florence was to marry me, and I had hopes of producing an heir within the year, should God have permitted it. Why should I do something so foolish as to bet my entire fortune, knowing that it could be lost in a moment? I would never have permitted myself to be so foolish, so very unwise."

Realizing that he had done nothing but talk, William forced his lips together. The urge to say more - as though to suggest that many words would convince her - grew forcefully, but he kept his lips clamped shut. Glancing towards Miss Lawrence, he saw her eyes fix themselves to the path in front of them, as a line drew itself between her brows. She was frowning hard, chewing at her lip as she considered all that he had said. William could not imagine her thoughts, but he assumed that there were many, each clamoring to be heard.

If she does not believe me, then there can be no arrangement between us.

He did not think that Miss Lawrence would play him false, and tell him that she trusted every word when in her mind she did not. The desperation in William's heart for her to believe that he spoke the truth about what had taken place spoke with such a loud volume that he wanted to cry out aloud, grasp her hand, and beg her to trust him. He was suddenly desperate not to lose her.

"I will admit that a gentleman willing to throw away his fortune for a game of cards does seem very strange." The sheer relief which came from hearing her speak so sent a rush of breath from William's lips. She glanced over at him and smiled briefly, but then looked away. "It must be very painful for you also to have society now treat you as though you are a gentleman with nothing but much foolishness in his heart."

A deep burning surfaced as William considered her words, revealing itself to him as though it had been hidden there for a long time, but only showing itself to him now.

"Yes, I believe that is true."

"Then I hope that it is of a small comfort if I state that I believe every word you have said." Again, Miss Lawrence smiled, but her eyes were still dark with many shadows. "Surely our first action ought to be to talk with Lord Gillespie, since he is the one who sent all of you to that gambling den in the first place."

"I had the very same thought but alas, Lord Gillespie is dead." Miss Lawrence let out a gasp of horror, and William cursed himself silently for speaking so bluntly. "Forgive me, I did not mean –"

"He is dead?" Miss Lawrence's eyes widened. "Then surely there is an even greater concern?"

"What do you mean?"

Her hand tightened on his arm.

"Surely there is now a chance that you yourself are in danger, and by continuing to search for whoever it was who did such a thing, you are putting yourself into harm's way. What if you find yourself in the same situation as Lord Gillespie?"

It was not a situation William had ever considered, and yet the more he thought of it, the more he realized that Miss Lawrence had an excellent point. There was a little more danger here than he had perhaps thought.

"You had not thought of such a thing before."

"No, I had not." William found himself reaching across to press her hand as they continued to walk together. "You cannot know how much of a relief it is to hear you say that you trust me - and now to hear your wisdom when it comes to considering my situation!"

"I hope I will be of some aid to you, but what can be done next? What can be your recourse, now that Lord Gillespie can be of no aid to you?"

William opened his mouth to answer, but quickly shut it again. The truth was that he had not even considered such a thing, having found himself confused and thinking mostly of Miss Lawrence herself.

"I... I do not know."

Inwardly, William realized just how foolish he must appear. He had no plan of what he could do next.

If this is so very important to me, why do I have no answer?

"I can understand that you are, of course, struggling against shock and great dismay." Miss Lawrence did not appear to express any such doubts over his wisdom... or lack thereof. "Might I ask if Lord Gillespie had any close acquaintances whom you might speak with?" Turning sharply, she grasped his arm with her free hand, her eyes suddenly bright. "Was he courting anyone?"

William blinked.

"That is an excellent suggestion. I believe that he was, yes." Squeezing his eyes closed, he tried to remember the young lady's name, all too aware of Miss Lawrence's grasping hand. She was waiting for him to answer, and he was struggling to remember the young woman's name. "A Miss...." He shook his head. "No, it was not Miss Messer. Now I recall!" His eyes flew open, and he saw Miss Lawrence smiling back at him. "She is Lady Sarah, daughter of the Earl of Gainsborough."

"Then I can speak with Lady Sarah. If Lord Gillespie has any close acquaintances, then might I suggest you speak with them? I do not know what you can discover, but it may be that at one time or another, Lord Gillespie said something of importance."

"That may very well be the case." William's heart soared as his hand found hers, pressing her fingers lightly. "Thank you, Miss Lawrence." The hope he had lost was now returning to him, for he had a way forward at last, thanks to her wisdom. "I am very grateful to you, Miss Lawrence."

A gentle flush edged itself across her cheeks, but she did not look away from him.

"I am only glad that I can be of aid to you, Lord Foster. After all, that is what I must do, is it not?"

Reminding himself that this was nothing more than an arrangement, and he ought not to allow his heart any overwhelming feelings as regarded the lady, William nodded, releasing her hand and dropping his own back to his side as he gave her a brief smile.

"I should return you to your mother. Whether or not she has noticed your absence, I feel duty bound to take you back to her."

Miss Lawrence did not move with him. Instead, she remained where she was, holding his arm still.

"When will I see you again?"

William blinked, and to his surprise, his heart filled with a warmth that seemed to seep through every pore. It took him a moment to form any response, such was his surprise.

"I... I had not thought." Her smile faded, and something stabbed through William's heart. "Allow me to return home and ensure that my invitation to tomorrow evening's ball is still present, and then I shall write to you to state whether or not I will be able to meet you there or not. If I am unable to attend, then I will make another arrangement, so that we might walk together again. Would that suit you?"

Miss Lawrence nodded, although she did not smile. William found himself almost desperate for the gentle smile to return to her lips, wanting to watch the way her eyes lit up, but he was not to have his wish granted. Miss Lawrence dropped her hand from his arm, and they stood apart, looking back at each other for a few moments.

Then she began to walk along the path, and he had no other choice but to follow her, cursing himself silently for bringing a look of sorrow to her face. They said nothing more until they returned to the place where they had first met. With a murmur of farewell, Miss Lawrence made her way back to her mother. William let himself watch her as she departed, eager for her to look back over her shoulder towards him so that he might smile, nod or wave. But he was to be disappointed again. She did not so much as glance back at him, walking forward with her back straight and her head held high. Frustration built in his heart as Lady Black-ford and Miss Henrietta did not even throw a look towards Miss Lawrence as she drew near, for they were much too busy in conversation with other gentlemen. She did not deserve to be treated in such a fashion, but yet what could he say? He could not go over to them and demand that they pay attention to Miss Lawrence. No, the only thing he could do was turn away in frustration and make his way home.

CHAPTER EIGHT

"Who was it you were walking with?"

Alice looked at her sister.

"What do you mean?"

"You may think that no one is watching, but I saw you yesterday." Henrietta's eyes narrowed. "You may believe that I was not observing you, but I can assure you, *dear* sister, that I saw everything. I saw you take your leave. I saw you walk away. I saw you return."

"There is no need for you to pry into my private affairs." Alice was not intimidated by her sister's attempts to appear threatening. "The truth is, Henrietta, that I was walking with a gentleman for a short while during the fashionable hour. I can assure you that mother remained in our sight at all times."

This last part, however, was a complete fabrication. Alice had no knowledge as to whether or not she had been able to see her mother during her walk with Lord Foster. She had not cared, just as her mother, in turn, had not cared either as to where Alice might be.

"It is a strange circumstance indeed to see *you* walking

with a gentleman." Henrietta's remark was meant to sear Alice, but she did not so much as flinch. "I was quite astonished! Imagine a gentleman finding any reason to be interested in your company."

That final remark, however, stung - despite Alice's strong resolve against allowing herself to react to such harsh words. Henrietta's cruelty cut at her, but she did not allow a single flash of pain to edge its way across her features. It was best that Henrietta did not know that there was any injury, otherwise, no doubt, she would use such words again... and again and again, repeatedly, for the sheer joy of injuring Alice.

"I shall tell Mama."

A nudge of worry entered Alice's heart, but she merely shrugged.

"To inform her of what, pray tell? To inform her that I was walking with a gentleman?" Laughing softly, she shook her head, making no attempt to keep the irony from her voice. "Walking with a gentleman? How very daring of me." Henrietta's lips twisted. "I am all too aware, dear sister, that you have no expectation of me ever finding a suitor, but it seems that your expectations may be disappointed. Perhaps I *shall* find a suitor and, mayhap, even a husband."

"You certainly shall not be courted before I am." Henrietta's chin lifted, her eyes sparkling with disdain. "This is your second Season. Your first was entirely unsuccessful, and I am quite certain that your second year will be just as fruitless as the first. This gentleman, whoever he is, will have no interest in you once he realizes who your sister is. Clearly, he has never been introduced to me before, but that is something which can be easily rectified."

The sheer arrogance in her sister's voice sent Alice's spirits tumbling. Was it possible that Henrietta would do whatever she could to make certain that such a thing would take place? Alice was all too aware that Henrietta could turn any gentleman's head... and his heart, if she wished it.

Lord Foster would never consider Henrietta.

There was a specific arrangement between herself and Lord Foster. It was a strange one, certainly, but there was a mutual trust. Henrietta could do or say whatever she pleased, but Alice was not about to believe her. Her assurance slowly returned, and she threw a hard glance at her sister.

"You must have a great deal of confidence in yourself, Henrietta, to say such a thing as that. Thankfully, I have even *more* confidence in my particular gentleman. He will not be swayed by such a selfish, arrogant creature as you."

Refusing to give her sister another single moment of her attention, Alice rose and made her way from the drawing room, turning her feet in the direction of her bedchamber, only to be stopped by the maid.

"You have a note, Miss."

A little surprised at the thrill of excitement that ran through her, Alice took it with a murmur of thanks. She did not need to ask who it was from, for only one person would be writing to her at present.

Hurrying to her bedchamber, she closed the door tightly before breaking the seal. Her heart quickened further still as she read the few short lines from Lord Foster. Yes, he would be present this evening at the ball. Again, he would be remaining as inconspicuous as he could, unwilling to step into society. He finished by mentioning that Lady Sarah would be present also, for he had heard from an acquaintance that her father and mother, who were both invited to the ball, had every expectation of attending. It would be an excellent opportunity for Alice, therefore, to speak with the young lady.

Alice nodded to herself, a slight rush of anxiety in her veins. Lord Foster's story was a strange one indeed, for to hear that he had been in some sort of inebriated state, without actually being inebriated, was a difficult thing to accept. But it had been the fervor in his green eyes which had convinced her of the truth. It was as though she could see written on his expression just how desperate he was for her to believe him. As she had considered it, Alice had thought about just how alone Lord Foster must be at present, placing herself in his situation and seeing the pain which would follow from being pushed away from society. Her heart had softened, and she had agreed to trust him and believe that his story was true. Even now, she could recall the waves of relief that had poured into his features as he had looked back at her. His shoulders had dropped, and his exhalation of breath had been swiftly followed by a smile. She was glad of it. She only prayed she would be able to help him in some way, for this was a very great tangle indeed.

"My dear Lady Florence. How well you look!".

To her surprise, Lady Florence looked a good deal happier than Alice had seen her in some time. There was color in her cheeks and her eyes appeared rather brighter, as though she found enjoyment in almost every moment that passed.

"I admit that I feel quite enlivened this evening! I find that I can complain about nothing, for this ball is utterly magnificent, is it not?"

"Good gracious, you *are* in good spirits." Smiling, Alice tilted her head so that she could see her friend a little better. "Perhaps you have found a little happiness?"

Lady Florence laughed.

"It is because I have taken your advice, and it is going very well! My father is now considering a *particular* gentleman, which has made my heart so very glad indeed. He is to call upon me tomorrow!"

"Then I am very happy for you, and I am glad that there are no lasting effects from your situation with Lord Foster."

"Certainly, there are not. In fact, I believe there is nothing but encouragement at present. I am very happy, although I will say that I am sorry for Lord Foster. His strange story did not leave me unaffected. It must be rather difficult for him, for very few want to have his company now, unless it is solely to bring a little more gossip about whatever event of theirs he attends."

They began to wander together through the ballroom, not going in any one particular direction.

"That is very true." Alice bit her lip, silently wondering whether or not she ought to tell her friend the truth. "I will beg of you to keep this a secret between us for the moment, but I am being courted by Lord Foster."

Lady Florence stopped. She stared straight ahead for a few moments, then slowly turned her head to look directly at Alice.

"You will think me ridiculous, I am sure, but I have no other option."

"You... you are teasing me." Red billowed into Lady Florence's face. "He is a disgraced gentleman!"

"And I have no hope of marriage! I have said that I will do all I can to aid him in regaining his fortune and in turn, he will take me as his bride. You must understand that there is nothing between us and that there never has been. I would never have considered him had it not been for these particular circumstances. It is only because he found himself in such a difficult situation that I began to wonder whether or not it could be useful for both of us. I do not want to become a companion. I do not want to have no chance of a future other than the one my father has dictated for me. I do hope that you can understand that."

Lady Florence blinked rapidly and shook her head.

"Goodness." Her breath rushed out as she closed her eyes. "I will confess myself to be a little overcome with surprise at this news, but also to state that I do not think that wise for you, my dear friend." Lady Florence opened her eyes, then reached out and grasped Alice's hand. "He is a disgraced gentleman with no fortune. I have no understanding of what you mean when you say that you seek to recover it, but surely a future with very little coin, and the requirement for employment is a very bleak future indeed."

That was true.

"I cannot disagree with you. I will not pretend it will not be difficult if such a thing should take place. But I would rather have a husband and the possibility of children over the requirement to become a companion to my aunt, even if I am faced with hardship. Of the two, I would choose a life with Lord Foster over that of servitude. And what should become of me once my employment to my aunt came to an end?" Shrugging her shoulders, she spread her hands. "I would be forced to cast myself upon my father's mercy or, if not his, then that of my sister and whoever her husband might be." From the drop of Lady Florence's eyebrows, Alice knew that she finally understood. "Do you truly believe that such a thing would be the better choice?"

Lady Florence closed her eyes and Alice was certain

that she was about to throw a great protest back at her. But much to her astonishment, when Lady Florence opened her eyes again, there was nothing but glassy tears there.

"You do not deserve to be treated so." Squeezing her hand gently, she shook her head. "Your father and mother should be giving you the same opportunities as they provide for the supposedly gifted Henrietta. I wish you did not have to make such a choice."

"It is not something which troubles me too much, now that I have the hope of a future with Lord Foster."

"But it is not a secure hope." Lady Florence held her gaze steadily. "My dear friend, if it was in my power to give you a great fortune so that you and Lord Foster could find happiness together, then I would do so."

Touched, Alice smiled gently.

"I know that you would, but pray do not concern yourself too much. Instead, you might pray that Lord Foster will regain his fortune and that I will be able to stand by his side as his wife, and mistress of his house. Pray that our future will be a secure one, that we will not linger in poverty. And if all else fails..." She licked her lips. "Then pray that it will not be long before Lord Foster or myself find an employment worthy of us."

A single tear fell from Lady Florence's eyes. She brushed it aside, but smiled, nonetheless.

"You have such a happiness in you, such a confidence in the face of doubts, that I cannot quite comprehend it, and I admire you greatly. I shall do as you ask. I shall pray that you are given all that you require, whether it be his fortune or-," she gulped. "Or employment."

"Thank you, my dear friend." Alice kept her lips in a smile. "I must now ask you whether or not you are acquainted with Lady Sarah? She was connected with Lord

Gillespie, who was acquainted with Lord Foster." Without going into her particular reasons for why she wished to speak with the lady, Alice shook her head at the questions in her friend's eyes. "I cannot tell you all, only that I must speak with her at once, for it may be of great use to Lord Foster."

"She is the daughter of Lord Gainsborough, is she not?"

"Yes, that is she."

"Then yes, I am acquainted with her. I believe she is here this evening. If you would like me to introduce you to her?" Nodding quickly, Alice waited as her friend looked around. "Come. Let us take a turn about the room."

Putting her arm through Alice's, Lady Florence led her across the ballroom and, without craning her neck or making it too obvious that she was searching for any sign of the lady, she soon managed to find her.

Alice looked into the eyes of a very pretty young lady, willowy in stature, with a head of golden curls and a delicate rosebud smile. She greeted Lady Florence warmly, then curtsied towards Alice.

"I am very pleased to make your acquaintance, Lady Sarah." Thinking quickly, Alice shook her head sadly. "I was very sorry to hear of the death of Lord Gillespie. I was told that you were closely acquainted with him."

Immediately, the smile which had been on Lady Sarah's face vanished. Her bright blue eyes widened slightly as she stared at Alice, who gave her nothing but a small smile in return. Lady Sarah blinked rapidly, then turned her head away, leaving Lady Florence and Alice to share a look.

"I did not know that a great many people knew of his passing as yet." Lady Sarah's voice was small. "Might you tell me how you came to hear of it?"

"I am acquainted with Lord Foster," Alice replied,

thinking it was best to be entirely honest. "He has spoken to me of it. Forgive me, I did not wish to upset you. Allow me to express my condolences."

Lady Sarah's lips trembled for a moment, but she gave Alice a rather wobbly smile.

"You have heard correctly. We *were* very closely acquainted and had our friendship continued, I believe that there would have been a future for us. I am only sorry that it can never be so now. His loss has affected my spirits greatly."

"As I can well imagine," Lady Florence murmured, as Alice nodded. "I too have recently lost a great hope, although not in the same way. I might add."

"Yes, I was sorry to hear of Lord Foster's foolishness." Lady Sarah let out a small sigh whilst Alice bit back a sharp response, finding herself eager to defend the gentleman. "That must have been a great disappointment to you, Lady Florence."

"It has been trying, yes. Thank you."

Not wishing to be drawn out of the conversation, Alice spoke up. The questions she had to ask Lady Sarah were a little blunt, but regardless, she knew she would have to ask them.

"It is most unusual to hear of a gentleman in the prime of his life losing it so early." Attempting to keep as much sympathy in her voice as possible, she spread both hands. "I do hope he did not bring his life to an end by his own foolishness. That would place an even greater burden on your soul."

Lady Sarah did not appear to be at all offended, answering Alice immediately with a shake of her head.

"It is worse than that. If you can believe it. Lord Gillespie's life was taken from him by another."

The gasp of shock from Alice was genuine.

"Are you quite certain?"

"Indeed I am." Lady Sarah's voice dropped as if she were wishing to speak confidentially. "It was very disturbing to hear such news, as you can imagine."

"And is there any knowledge as to who has done such a despicable thing?"

Alice glanced across at Lady Florence, silently relieved that her friend had been the one to ask the question, rather than herself.

Lady Sarah shook her head, her only response a sigh.

"Did he ever speak to you about those of his acquaintances who might wish him ill? Was there anyone in London who had a grudge against him?"

Lady Sarah sighed again, dropped her head, and ran fingers lightly across her eyebrows, as though speaking of such things was causing her great distress.

"He did not often speak to me about his business affairs, but there was one occasion where he was in great melancholy. I recall that he stated that a particular endeavor was not going particularly well, and he wished to remove himself from it."

"I wonder what sort of business that could be."

Alice let the question trickle from her lips, looking away so that Lady Sarah did not think she was asking her directly.

"I am afraid that he never gave me the particulars, although I am aware that there were other titled gentlemen involved."

"Do you know any of their names?" Catching Lady Sarah's wide-eyed, rather startled look, Alice quickly covered her question with an explanation. "I ask only because I thought it could be of aid to Lord Foster or to any other of Lord Gillespie's friends who might wish to find the man who took Lord Gillespie's life."

This seemed to satisfy Lady Sarah, for she nodded, and then after a few moments shook her head.

"I am afraid he did not give me any of their names. I do recall him mentioning a Viscount, but I cannot recall his title. I am sorry."

"You have nothing to apologize for," Alice assured her, smiling warmly. "I am aware that this must be incredibly painful for you to have to recount. I am certain that you would have enjoyed a happy future with Lord Gillespie, and I am sorry that the chance of such has been taken from you."

"You are very kind." Lady Sarah reached out and grasped Alice's hand. "It has been a painful loss, but the rest of the Season awaits - or my mother so tells me. And..." She dropped her gaze and Alice's hand. "There was no commitment between myself and Lord Gillespie. We were not even officially courting, although that was soon to come."

"I am certain that does not make your pain any less."

Alice's heart was full of sympathy and compassion for the young lady.

"No, it does not." Lady Sarah sighed, then smiled. "Pray, excuse me." Her gaze lingered over Alice's shoulder. "I can see that my mother is calling me. No doubt she has another gentleman she wishes to introduce me to."

A slightly rueful smile touched her lips, but she inclined her head and then excused herself from their company.

Lady Florence turned to look directly at Alice.

"My dear girl, is it possible that there could be any truth in Lord Foster's statement that his wealth was taken from him by unscrupulous means?"

Alice blinked, a little astonished at her friend's question.

"Whatever do you mean?"

"I can see where your questions to Lady Sarah are coming from. Having told me of your arrangement with Lord Foster, is it not now the case that you believe Lord Gillespie had something to do with his misfortune?"

Alice nodded.

"Lord Gillespie was the one who sent Lord Foster and the other gentlemen to the east side of London. *He* was the one who gave them the names of the gambling dens they visited, and for whatever reason, Lord Gillespie himself was unable to attend with them! That night, all six gentlemen found themselves robbed in one way or another - at least, that is what I believe took place." Alice gave her friend a brief smile. "I cannot see what Lord Gillespie's death has to do with Lord Foster's predicament, but I believe there may be a correlation."

Lady Florence shook her head, sighed, and pressed lightly at the bridge of her nose for a moment or two.

"I hope that you are not going to be in any danger."

Alice smiled and shrugged her shoulders.

"I am afraid I cannot say for certain, my dear friend. But I have promised to aid Lord Foster in whatever way I can, and I fully intend to do so." Catching sight of the very gentleman in question, her eyes widened slightly. "Forgive me, but I must go and speak to him. He is standing in the shadows but has been watching us speak with Lady Sarah, I think."

Lady Florence glanced over her shoulder, but evidently not seeing him, let her gaze return to Alice.

"Very well. I should like to know if you discover anything." A touch of pink came into her cheeks, and she pulled her gaze away. "It is not because I have any feelings for Lord Foster or wish that our betrothal continued, but it is more a mild curiosity. And, of course, I am eager to know that you will remain safe."

"I shall do so."

Giving her friend's hand a light squeeze, Alice made her way across the ballroom, heedless of her mother's presence and how far she stepped from it. Making her way to the edge of the room, she smiled as she approached Lord Foster. He was standing near the wall, his face half hidden in shadow, but he turned towards her a little more as she drew near.

"Miss Lawrence." Offering her a swift nod, he kept his hands behind his back. "I saw you speaking with Lady Sarah."

"Yes. Lord Gillespie and she were very close but were not yet betrothed, nor even courting. She seemed deeply upset at his loss, however. I believe that a betrothal would shortly have taken place had he not been snatched from her."

"A very difficult situation, I am sure."

Something flickered in his eyes and Alice took a step closer. From what she could see of his expression, his jaw was tight, and his eyes were searching her face as if he was desperate to know what it was that she had discovered, but yet was unwilling to press her.

"Lady Sarah told me very little, other than the fact that Lord Gillespie had spoken to her on occasion of a situation he found himself in. A situation that he wished to remove himself from, but where he was not permitted to do so. She believes it caused him a great deal of trouble."

"A situation he could not remove himself from?" A

frown darkened Lord Foster's eyes even further. "What do you mean?"

"A business situation, I believe. There were no particulars and, as much as I would like to offer you more, I cannot do so. I am afraid that she knew very little."

His shoulders dropped.

"That is better than nothing at all."

"Oh, there was one other thing which was mentioned. She did state that she believed there were other gentlemen involved in this business affair and that one of them was a Viscount."

Lord Foster snatched in a breath, stepped forward, and caught her arm, as a fervency filled his eyes. Her breath caught in her chest, and she looked back at him, a little mesmerized by his change in demeanor.

"A Viscount, you say?"

"Yes, Lord Foster."

Alice's heart began to quicken as his fingers wrapped around her arm a little more tightly. He was so very close to her, his breath brushing across her cheek, as if in a tender gesture.

"A sudden memory has just come back to me, Miss Lawrence." Lord Foster's eyes flared wide. "When you said that a Viscount had been involved, I recall now that the gentleman across the table from me on that fateful night was himself a Viscount."

"Are- are you quite certain?"

There was no mistaking the excitement and anticipation in Lord Foster's voice, but Alice wondered how he could be sure when his memory of the event was meant to be so very muddled.

Lord Foster moved closer still until his lips were only inches away from hers. No doubt it was so that they could speak in confidence, but Alice's skin prickled, and her pulse quickened at the nearness of him. A gentleman had never stood so close to her before. And now that Lord Foster did so, Alice found herself quite overwhelmed. Her mouth was dry, her tongue was feeling a little too large for her mouth, and thus she clamped her lips shut, refusing to say another word until her heart rate returned to normal.

"Yes, I am quite certain." Speaking in low tones, Lord Foster captured her gaze with his own. "It is only because you told me of that Viscount that I finally remember some details about the night. The man I played against made a few flippant remarks. I recall how he laughed, but his words remained muddled to me. However, now there is one thing that I do recall. I remember, he *stated* that he was a Viscount."

A curl of excitement began to twist Alice's stomach.

"That was before I ended up entirely unconscious, however. It was not until the following afternoon that I realized what I had lost."

Alice blinked.

"How did this man – this Viscount – steal your fortune from you?"

It was something she had never thought to ask, until now.

Lord Foster drew in a deep breath and pulled back a little, looking at her directly. There was a tightness about his jaw, as if he were upset at having to recall such a thing.

"I went to my solicitors. Upon speaking with them, they produced a note which had been signed and sealed by myself. The note stated that they were to give the bearer of that note a large amount of coin. However, the name of the fellow was neither required nor recorded." His mouth twisted to one side. "At least now I know, however, that he was a Viscount. That shall prove helpful, I am sure."

"Goodness." Alice waited as Lord Foster's gaze slowly returned to her. "Then what I have discovered *is* of significance."

"I should say so."

Being able to read the question on Lord Foster's lips before he even asked it, Alice shook her head.

"No, she knew nothing more. Lady Sarah could not recall any further details about this matter. I believe Lord Gillespie was deliberately vague when speaking to her." Immediately, Lord Foster looked away, his eyes dropping to the ground as a muscle in his jaw worked. His fingers fell from her arm, and Alice felt, suddenly, strangely alone. "But I do not think that you need to consider this thing most dreadful. Yes, there are many Viscounts in London, but Lord Gillespie would have only a few as his acquaintances and friends. I am sure that there is a way that we can discover which gentlemen were close to him."

Lord Foster's eyes lifted back to hers. The tightness in his jaw loosened and he slowly began to nod.

"Yes. Miss Lawrence. You are quite correct to say so." His eyes widened. "That is a wise thought." His hand grasped hers once more and fire burned up her arm. "A *very* wise thought."

"And it may help us to make significant progress."

Smiling warmly, Alice tried to move back, but Lord Foster had her fingers in his and he was holding on tightly. How had she not noticed his fingers lacing with hers?

"I shall speak to my friends and acquaintances in the hope that one of them will have known Lord Gillespie better than I."

Alice nodded.

"I am glad that you have found a little hope, and that the information Lady Sarah has offered us can be used to your advantage."

Instead of anxiety in his eyes, instead of dark dread, there was a flash of confidence. Alice's heart lifted as she smiled into his eyes.

"I have a thought."

Lord Foster bit his lip and looked away. The hope in his eyes had grown, but it appeared to have given way to something else.

"Yes, Lord Foster. What is it?"

Lord Foster shook his head.

"You may think this a little ridiculous... foolish even. But I had wondered about making my way into Lord Gillespie's house."

Alice caught her breath. All the warmth which had flooded her only a few moments ago faded immediately as she looked into his eyes. She could see that he meant every word.

"Why ever should you do something such as that?"

Her hand pulled out of his.

"I did not say that I *would* have to do so, but that I might consider it." Lord Foster shrugged. "Lord Gillespie will have left behind a lot of correspondence. I am beginning to wonder whether or not it would bring any light to my situation to look through his recent letters. Now that I know that a Viscount has been involved in this affair, then surely it would not take a great deal of effort to search through his recent correspondence in the hope of finding any letters from such a titled gentleman."

Fear clutched at Alice's heart, and she shook her head, mute.

"You think it an unfavorable idea?"

"More than a little unfavorable, my Lord. I think it's rather foolish."

His eyebrows lifted.

"Foolish?"

She nodded to him.

"Yes, foolish. What if you were discovered? What could be your excuse for being found in the home of a dead man?"

"I would not permit myself to be caught." Lord Foster smiled, but there was a stiffness to it. "You may think the risk is great, but I can see no other way forward. Yes, I could ask many people about Lord Gillespie's friends and the name of particular Viscounts he kept in company with - but what answers could they give me? They could give me the names of ten Viscounts and I would be none the wiser! But if I were to look through his correspondence, then I might find myself with an answer more quickly than any amount of questioning might manage to provide me with one."

Lord Foster held her gaze steadily, but Alice could only shake her head again.

This did not seem a wise plan at all. To her mind, if Lord Foster was caught, then his reputation would be damaged all the more. The *ton* would state that, as an impoverished fellow, he had gone in the hope of seeking a little additional wealth - anything he could take from Lord Gillespie's house. Anything that would bring him a little bit of coin. Any explanation he tried to give would be thrown aside.

"I seek only to protect you, Lord Foster."

"There is no need for you to do so. I am perfectly able to take care of my own situation."

There was a flash of temper in his eyes and Alice bristled as he folded his arms across his already puffed-out chest.

"I am doing what I have promised, Lord Foster. I am attempting not only to aid you but to preserve your reputation as best as I can." Her temper flared, and she found herself saying something she had never intended. "If you are determined to go, then I shall come with you."

Lord Foster immediately shook his head.

"No, Miss Lawrence, I couldn't let you do such a thing."

"And yet I am determined." Realizing that she could not change her mind, and state that she would not go with him after all, Alice held her head high. "If we went together, then perhaps I might be able to protect you from any lingering servants... or any of the gentry who may come into his house for whatever reason. Or mayhap even his successor!"

"Miss Lawrence, when we made our agreement, I did not ever think nor expect that you would go to such lengths as this."

Giving him a small smile, Alice stepped forward just so that she was as close to him as he had been to her. A hint of spice caught her nose and she inhaled instinctively, finding her stomach dropping, before it ricocheted back up, something delicious swirling through it. Speaking in a somewhat shaky voice, she held her gaze fixed to his.

"I will not be put off, Lord Foster. If you are determined to go to Lord Gillespie's house, then I shall go with you, and together we will look through his correspondence to see what we can discover. Now what say you? Will you accept my offer, or will you refuse?"

Lord Foster said nothing for some moments. The air seemed to crackle as she looked up into his face, never blinking, never looking away. And then he dropped his head, speaking to her in a low whisper which had every inch of her shivering.

It seems that I am to wed a determined young woman." A hint of a smile touched his lips. "I do not know whether I ought to be pleased or irritated. But yes, if you are determined to join me, then I see no way forward other than to agree. I do not know how you will do it, Miss Lawrence, for your parents will surely miss you if you are absent from the house. But it must be done so – either by one or both of us."

The tone of his voice did nothing to prevent Alice's determination. It had wavered a little, but at the challenge in his eyes and in his voice, she found it renewed.

"You need not have any concern as to how I will go about it, Lord Foster." Placing both hands on her hips, she tipped her chin up. "Tell me when I must be there, and I shall meet you at Lord Gillespie's."

"Very well." Lord Foster grinned, and the expression on his face was so startling that Alice's eyes cleared and her breath hitched. How had he flitted from one expression to the next with such swiftness?

"Let us say Friday." Lord Foster's voice was low, and to her utter astonishment, his fingers lifted to trace across her cheek and down the curve of her neck to rest upon her shoulder. "I did not think you so determined, Miss Lawrence. It is something of a surprise to me, but I do not think it is an unwelcome one." The grin began to fade, and Alice finally took a breath, then let out a small gasp as his nearness suddenly overwhelmed her, to the point that she was struggling to think anything comprehensible. Licking her lips, she let her gaze rest on his mouth for a moment, seeing how his lips puckered. Would there ever come a time when he would kiss her? Would there ever be a moment when she would lose herself in his embrace? "I shall send you a note tomorrow."

Lord Foster stepped back sharply, and everything

between them fell away. Alice was returned to the moment, to the dancing, and the conversation and laughter which filled the room, instead of the silence which had overwhelmed her as she had looked up into Lord Foster's face. Turning completely away from him, unwilling to look up any longer, Alice tried to steady her furious heart. These few minutes in his company had sent her into a whirlwind of emotions, and she was not entirely ready to return to herself. She did not hear Lord Foster bid her farewell, nor did she see him take his leave of her. Instead, she looked out unseeingly at the crowd, leaning back against the wall of the ballroom and taking deep breaths over and over until she finally felt settled.

This is only a practical arrangement. I cannot allow emotions to confuse matters further.

Closing her eyes, Alice pressed one hand to her stomach. It would do her no good to think of Lord Foster in any other way than she did at present. To fall in love with him would cause all manner of problems, she was quite sure... and they had problems enough already.

CHAPTER NINE

There was a moment when you almost kissed her.

William's thoughts tore at him, and he shook his head to himself. If he was being entirely honest, then yes, he would admit that he had almost pressed a kiss upon Miss Lawrence's willing lips. Relieved that he had not done so, he had stepped away from the ballroom with his feelings in complete disarray.

Sighing to himself, he pushed one hand through his hair and dropped his head. It was just as well he had not done so, for he had no intention of allowing any feelings to arise when it came to Miss Lawrence. The situation was already difficult, and it would offer very little help to either of them to make it all the more confusing.

Dropping his hand, he brought his thoughts back to the present and looked again towards Lord Gillespie's house. He had been standing quietly, studying it, for the last hour, but thus far there appeared to be no signs of life. There were no flickering candles in the windows, and given that dusk was soon approaching, he would have expected there to be at least one or two lights if anyone was in the house.

The front door was firmly closed, the knocker had been removed from the door, and no servants had been seen at any of the windows. To William's mind, it appeared that Lord Gillespie's servants were no longer in the house and that no one had come as yet to sort through Lord Gillespie's things – or to claim the house itself.

Frowning, William tilted his head. He assumed that Lord Gillespie had a younger brother who would take on the title, but such things could take some time, which meant it would be best for him to search the house as soon as possible.

Although this does beg the question of how I am to get inside.

It was not something he had given much thought to. His consideration had been solely on what he would do once he had entered Lord Gillespie's study, rather than how he was to get inside in the first place. Grimacing, he pressed his lips flat against each other, thinking hard. Perhaps a window or a door to the servants' entrance would be a little ajar, or even better, left unlocked in the shock and confusion after Lord Gillespie's death. Mayhap he could just fiddle with a window lock a little, in the hope that it would permit him entry - although he could not imagine Miss Lawrence climbing through a window in a flurry of skirts. A grin spread across his face as he pictured it, which was then swiftly followed by a rush of heat when he thought of what such an action might reveal.

"Have you been waiting for long?"

William jumped as Miss Lawrence's voice reached his ears. He had been so lost in his thoughts that he had not seen her approaching. The burning heat in his frame doubled as he coughed, trying to regain his composure.

"You appear a little surprised to see me." Miss

Lawrence's eyes looked back at him steadily. "Did you truly believe that I would not join you this afternoon? Did you think that I would change my mind and decide to remain home with my mama? I have a greater stubbornness of character than that."

It took William a moment to reply, given that he was struggling with tugging his thoughts away from what he had pictured, his heart still beating furiously. Such a thought had been none too proper and now that he was faced with the object of this unusual, unexpected desire, he was not quite certain what to say. Coughing, he dropped his head for a moment, hoping that he would soon be able to forget such a thing if he was not looking at her.

"I was focusing entirely on watching Lord Gillespie's house," he told her, his voice rasping. "That is all."

"I see." From the slight curl of her mouth, William was not sure that she believed him. "And have you seen anything of importance?"

William nodded at the house.

"It appears that there is no one present there." Whenever he could, he pulled his eyes from hers, for looking at her seemed to send his thoughts into turmoil. "I am going to wait until it becomes a little darker and then make my way towards the servants' entrance."

"And that is how we are to enter, is it?"

Shrugging as nonchalantly as he could, William threw her a brief smile.

"I am hopeful that we shall find a way in, yes."

It was not unexpected when Miss Lawrence narrowed her eyes.

"You have no direct plan as to how we are to enter Lord Gillespie's house?"

"I am certain we shall find a way." Easing confidence

into his voice, William gave her a brief smile. "Are you certain that your absence will not be noticed? Where are your mother and sister this evening?"

Much to his surprise, Miss Lawrence gave a brief laugh.

"Lord Foster, I am very good at being invisible." Her laugh was not a pleasant one, but rather one that tried to hide pain. "I will show you. I will cross the road and walk directly towards Lord Gillespie's entrance, and no one will even glance in my direction."

She did not wait for his permission, nor his agreement, but strode across the road, walking past three other gentlemen - none of whom looked at her - and then turned directly towards Lord Gillespie's townhouse. No one turned their head towards her. The last thing William saw was her head disappearing as she walked down the stone steps that led to the servants' entrance.

With a mutter of frustration, he hurried after her, dropping his head as he walked past the same three gentlemen. One of them murmured something that sounded like his name, but he ignored it. A quick glance over his shoulder told him that none were looking back at him, and he scurried quickly down the stone steps - but there was no sign of Miss Lawrence. His heart began to quicken as he looked around, wondering where she could have gone, in what was a very small space. Had he lost her? His heart began to pound as memories of finding Lord Gillespie's body returned to his mind. Was Miss Lawrence in the same situation? Was the man who had killed Lord Gillespie now returned to snatch away Miss Lawrence? It made very little sense, but the fear drove itself directly into William's heart, and for a moment he could not breathe.

And then the servants' door opened.

"Are you simply going to stand there gawping, or are you going to come in?"

Miss Lawrence's eyes danced as she smiled at him. William's breath was pouring out of him in heaving gasps, and he found his hand grasping hers as they stepped into the silent house. She was close to him now. The smile in her eyes faded as she searched his face, evidently seeing the concern which had filled him only moments ago.

"I am quite all right. I noticed that the latch was a little loose, and it did not take long for it to open to my prying fingers... and a hair pin."

She smiled at him, but William did not return the smile, his fingers tight on hers, panic stealing every other emotion from him.

"I thought you might have been..." Closing his eyes, he dropped his head and squeezed her hand as if wanting to make quite certain that she was still very much alive. "This house holds a dark memory for me, Miss Lawrence. I feared that the same person who had overtaken Lord Gillespie had taken you also."

"But they have not."

Her hand pulled from his as he opened his eyes, but it was not so that she could draw away. Rather, her fingers brushed down his cheek, her eyes fixing themselves to his as she spoke with a confidence that chased away his fear. William said nothing for some moments, looking back into her face, seeing her searching eyes, and finding his heart beginning to beat all the more quickly - although it was not for the same reason as before. His shuddering breath warned him that he was losing his devotion to the task at hand and becoming distracted by something entirely unexpected. With an effort, he pulled his remaining fingers from hers, nodded, and then turned away. Fire burned across his cheek, where she had run her fingers over his skin, and when it began to diminish, disappointment filled William's heart. The urge to draw close to her again was an almost impossible desire to deny but he strode through the servants' quarters with determination, unwilling to allow himself to become preoccupied. Miss Lawrence had come here of her own behest, but he still had a responsibility, as a gentleman, to make certain that no harm came to her. He would not do anything that would be considered untoward, despite the strange urgency in his heart for him to do so. Her footsteps clattered behind him as he claimed the staircase which led them from the servants' quarters to the main rooms.

"What if there is someone within? What shall we say?"

"I do not know." Glancing over his shoulder, William gave her a grim smile. "There is very little excuse one can give for being found in the home of a dead man." When he caught her eyes, he saw her smile at him, and his emotions tore themselves into a thousand pieces and rearranged themselves again. "Are you quite certain you wish to be here, Miss Lawrence?"

"Yes, of course. My determination is as strong as yours." Letting out a huff of breath, she set her shoulders. "We are to make our way to his study now, yes? Do you know which room it is?" William nodded as a shudder ran through his frame - a shudder that Miss Lawrence saw for she grasped his hand with hers. "Lord Foster?"

"It is where I found him." Taking in a deep breath, he remained holding her fingers. "Come, it is this way."

The house did not appear at all welcoming. It was dark with air that smelled of dust and silence. No candles were lit, and the growing darkness spread its hold over the house. Ignoring his rolling stomach, William opened the study door and pushed his way inside, half expecting to see Lord Gillespie still slumped over his desk. He let out a ragged breath as he took in the room, and Miss Lawrence came to stand next to him, her presence a comfort. There was, of course, no one there. The blood had been cleaned but there was still a metallic smell that bit the back of William's throat.

"We are to search for some documents relating to that Viscount, are we not?" Miss Lawrence released his hand. "His correspondence?"

Her practical remarks pulled William from his despondency.

"Yes." Taking in a deep breath, he strode towards the desk, pushing out any images which remained there of what he had seen before. "Any documents or letters which pertain to *any* Viscount must be taken with us. We might read them and then leave them here I suppose, but I have no wish to linger any longer than is necessary. If required, I can return and replace them at a later time."

"Very well." Miss Lawrence stepped closer to the desk and began to open the drawers. William himself turned to another chest of drawers and began to search through them carefully, wincing at every sound. He did not think that there would be anyone within the house, but all the same he felt a little nervous that they could be discovered. It would be one thing to be found with Miss Lawrence entirely unchaperoned, but quite another to be discovered in the late Lord Gillespie's rooms, searching through his things.

"I think I have found something."

Miss Lawrence's voice caught William's attention and he turned to her

"What is it?"

Miss Lawrence did not look at him but continued to read the paper in her hand.

"I believe this is in reference to the scheme in East London," she murmured, her eyes filled with shadows as she frowned. "Look, it speaks of the gentlemen whom he will send there."

She did not hand him the letter, but held it still, leaning towards him as she spoke, her other hand pointing out the reference she had just made. William found himself leaning into her he tried to concentrate on the letter. She was so close to him, and given that he was still confused over his strange reaction to the thought of losing her, he found himself struggling with his lack of concentration. Miss Lawrence glanced at him.

"What do you think?"

Tilting his head, William shrugged, nodded, and opened his mouth to speak only for a sudden clanging sound to ripple up through the silence of the house towards him. In the next second, Miss Lawrence had stuffed the letter into her pocket and William was scurrying towards the other side of the room, tidying away what he had been looking through. The noise came again as though someone was opening and closing doors and William's heart began to pound furiously as he looked around the room for somewhere for them to hide.

Miss Lawrence's wide eyes met his and they stared at each other for a long moment. Her eyes were huge, her face pale, and William could only shake his head, wordlessly, struggling to think of where they might go. The sound came again, and Miss Lawrence jerked visibly, closing her eyes before she turned around and moved to the left of the room. The large curtains which hung from the windows gave her an adequate hiding space. Every sense was alive with panic as William threw himself towards a large chest in the corner of the room. Flinging open the lid, he was relieved to see that it was entirely empty and hurried to climb inside, letting the lid close on him just as the door to the study opened. His heart was pounding so furiously that he could barely hear anything else. Muffled voices reached him, but he could make nothing out. Whoever it was in the house was looking for something, just as he and Miss Lawrence had been. Could this be the Viscount? Could this be the man who had stolen so much from him? A sudden wish to fling back the lid came over him, but he resisted the urge. It was not until silence had filled the room again that he dared to crack the lid a little. Nobody was there. He could hear no other noises and prayed silently that whoever had been present was now quite gone from the house.

"Miss Lawrence." Whispering her name, he removed himself from the chest. "Miss Lawrence, you may come out now. They are gone."

She did not reply. Making his way slowly across the room so that he would not accidentally make any floorboards creak, William pulled back the curtain. No doubt Miss Lawrence was a little afraid and perhaps she was curled up in a ball on the floor, using the curtains as a flimsy shield.

Horror tore through him as he realized she was no longer there.

Whirling around, William stared from one object in the room to the next, as if he thought she might somehow just be standing there. Had she changed her hiding place? No, that could not be. There had not been enough time for her to do so, and besides, where exactly would she have gone? Panic began to build as he pushed one hand through his hair, his hands going to his hips as he stared around the room. Closing his eyes, he blew out a long breath, realizing with even more dread that she was the one who held the letter. He had not even had the opportunity to read the name of the Viscount involved, but if that letter had any significance whatsoever, then perhaps that was why Miss Lawrence was no longer present with him. She had been taken. Whoever had been in this room and found her, had taken the letter and her with them.

Then I cannot simply leave her to her fate.

Yes, there were still more letters to be searched, more correspondence to go through, but none of that mattered at the present moment. The only thing in William's thoughts was Miss Lawrence. Hurtling from the study, his feet pounded across the floor as he ran the length of the hallway and down the servants' staircase. The evening air cooled his hot face but did nothing to calm him.

Frantic, he looked to his left and his right as he searched desperately for even a hint of where Miss Lawrence might now be. He could see nothing. The shadows of dusk were beginning to capture London already and only added to the darkness beginning to swirl through his heart.

I ought to have been stronger. I ought to have demanded that she remain at home rather than join me here.

Guilt pierced him, but William held willingly onto the pain. He had done this. By his foolishness, he had allowed this to happen and now, it seemed, Miss Lawrence was gone and there was nothing he could do to protect her from whatever evil fate now befell her.

CHAPTER TEN

I can only pray that Lord Foster forgives me.

Walking as quickly as she could, but keeping her eyes downcast, Alice hurried after the one gentleman she hoped would offer Lord Foster some sort of answer, the gentleman who had been in the room while she and Lord Foster had been hiding. He was not someone she recognized but, at present, she had no other thought than to follow him, quite certain that he was somehow involved in Lord Gillespie's death - and may have pulled Lord Foster's fortune from his unwilling hands. Why else would such a person be in the study of a dead man? Through a slight chink in the curtains, she had watched as the gentleman and his servant had searched through the very same documents that she and Lord Foster had been looking through a short while before. The first gentleman was rather small and scrawny, with a darkness in his expression that made her shudder. The second man, the man she assumed to be his servant, was broad-shouldered, with a great deal of strength to his frame. She did not want to imagine what such a fellow might do, should she be discovered, and yet that had not been warning enough for her to stay away from them both. Having very little idea as to where Lord Foster had hidden, Alice had not had any opportunity to search for him, fearful that the two men would escape from her if she lingered. Whispering to him that she was going after them, she had slipped from the room and followed the two intruders.

Which was precisely what she was still doing now. The gentlemen had seemed to not have a carriage, for he walked with great purpose and did not slow down for a single moment. Whether or not they had been able to find anything of importance in Lord Gillespie's study, Alice was unable to tell. The letter she held in her pockets, however, might well be the one they had been looking for. Her fingers stole to her pockets, and she touched the corner of the letter gently, a little concerned that somehow it had gone missing in her hurry. To her relief, it was still there.

At this moment it is something of a blessing to be rather invisible.

A wry smile tugged at her lips as the two gentlemen turned and made their way into a gentlemen's club. The smaller man walked directly inside while the second turned to stand beside it, his hands clasped behind his back. Alison ducked her head, hiding her face, and hurried past them, quite certain that the broad-shouldered man would not so much as glance at her. Daring a look herself, she turned her head over her shoulder, but the fellow was not watching her. He stared directly ahead, evidently waiting for his master's return, and willing to protect him in the interim from any unwanted guests.

Alice hesitated, slowing her steps as she came to a corner, unwilling to walk around it for fear that she would lose sight of this man. Crossing the quiet road on quick feet, she looked back towards him.

I have very little idea as to whether or not his master will return before the evening is out.

Lifting one finger to her mouth, she tapped at her lips a moment, trying to think of what she could do. It was early in the evening still, and no doubt the gentleman inside, being a member of the *ton*, would find something to occupy himself. Perhaps he had an invitation to some ball or another, or mayhap he would spend the entirety of his evening in the gentlemen's club. What was she to do? Stand on the corner and wait for him to emerge? She could very easily miss him, and with that awareness came another dark thought - that standing alone on a street corner was not wise for a young lady. A greater danger could overtake her.

And yet she did not want to lose sight of this fellow. To return to Lord Foster, only to tell him that she had followed the man but did not know anything about either him or his servant would be a spectacular failure. She forced herself to drop her hand to her side, to stand calmly, even as an edge of panic began to rise in her heart. She would have to do *something*.

Her eyes flared as she realized with relief that this particular gentlemen's club would surely have a ledger containing the names of the gentleman who came and went on any particular night. All she needed to do was to find out the name of this establishment, and Lord Foster could do the rest. After all, she knew the day, and near enough the time, that this gentleman had entered the establishment. It would not take much for Lord Foster to discover his name, surely.

Taking a deep breath, Alice nodded to herself. A little irritated that she had not taken note of the name on the sign as she had walked past, she gathered her strength and began to walk along the street once more, crossing the road to the other side. The broad-shouldered man was still standing there, silent and foreboding and, as she walked past him, his hand reached out and grasped her shoulder.

"Release me!"

Her skin crawled with fright as his fingers tightened on her shoulder all the more. She had tried to speak with great firmness, but Alice's face burned at the weakness of her voice as she spoke. She tried to twist away, but the man's fingers tightened, and he leaned toward her.

"This is the second time that you have walked past this establishment." A low voice made her shiver in fright. "You shall have no company here this evening. You shall not make a single penny from the gentlemen in this club. Might I suggest you take your... wares..." his dark eyes flickered down over her form and back again towards her eyes, "...elsewhere."

It took a moment for Alice to realize what he meant. The moment she did, however, such a heat overtook her that she felt as though she might burn up with sheer mortification. He thought her a lady of the night? She opened her mouth to correct him, only to snap it closed again. Perhaps she could use this to her advantage.

"You cannot blame young women such as myself for being eager. These men here will pay a high price."

A little relieved that the gloom would hide her hot cheeks, she let out a small breath of relief as the man lifted his hand from her shoulder.

"Be that as it may, you will get nothing here tonight."

She released what she hoped was a sorrowful sigh. "That is disappointing. Could you remind me of the name of this place, just so that I can tell my... friends not to bother coming here themselves? We have only a few short hours and I wouldn't like them to waste their time as I have done."

"That is very kind of you, I'm sure." The man's voice was a little lifted now, no longer as dark. "Or maybe you will send them here while you get your fill from their usual spots, no?" He chuckled and Alice tried to join in. "Well, you may tell your friends that they should avoid Donley's. The gentlemen here spend all of their hours inside and do not often emerge until they are quite ready to retire to bed... *without* company, I might add."

Another dark chuckle sent a thrill of horror down Alice's spine, but she forced a laugh regardless.

"How very kind you are." Forcing herself to play a part, she moved a little closer, her eyebrow lifting. "What about yourself? I could give you a penny or two less off the price since you've been so good to me."

The man grinned, a flash of white in the gloom.

"As *kind* an offer as that is, I've got my orders."

Alice let out what she hoped was a heavy sigh.

"That is a pity. I won't trouble you anymore."

Forcing her steps to be slow rather than the hurried rush her whole body desired, Alice took her time walking away from Donley's and the broad-shouldered man. Her heart was pounding so furiously that it seemed as though she could not find enough breath, for her chest grew tight and stars began to flicker in the edges of her vision.

You are safe, Alice.

Pausing for a moment, she took in deep breaths as one hand went to her heart. She had been more daring than she had ever expected herself to be. In one night, she had broken into a gentleman's house, hidden from unknown intruders, and pretended to be a lady of the night to garner particular information from a fellow standing outside a gentlemen's club. Despite the fear that she felt at this moment, it had been worth it.

All she had to do now was tell Lord Foster.

~

"ALICE, YOU HAVE A VISITOR."

Alice looked up from where she had been reading.

"Father?"

"A gentleman has come to call on you, Alice. A *disgraced* gentleman, I might add."

"You mean Lord Foster?" A little surprised that the gentleman had decided to call upon her at her father's house, Alice rose from her chair. "Thank you for telling me. I shall go to him at once."

Lord Blackford put out one hand as she made her way to the door.

"You shall never be permitted to take up with such a fellow." His eyes narrowed as Alice looked up at him, defiance building a fortress in her chest. "He is a gentleman disgraced. The *ton* rejects him. You must do the same."

"I have already accepted his offer, father," she told him plainly. "I am sure news of it is already spreading through the *ton* and I have no intention of turning my back on the gentleman." This was not the entirety of the truth, for as yet, they had not made any plan as to when they might decide to betroth themselves to each other, but given that it was soon to take place, she had no reason to keep such a thing back from her father. "We are betrothed, and I will marry him."

Immediately, Lord Blackford's hand reached out and grasped her arm tightly, tugging her forward. When she looked up at him, her father's face was dark with anger, but

Alice herself felt no fear. No doubt a good deal of her father's anger came from the fact that he was no longer able to have control over the situation, as he had expected. His attempts to send her to be a companion to his elderly sister would be flouted.

"You cannot have accepted him. I did not give you my permission."

"You did, Father." Alice stepped back so that his hand was forced to fall back to his side. "You stated that I should have to find myself a husband by the end of the Season and that is precisely what I have done. Lord Foster fully intends to marry me, and the date will be set soon enough."

Her father let out a furious exclamation, but he did not appear to know what to say. His eyes were wide as he stared at her, but Alice merely looked back at him. She was not about to be pulled from Lord Foster now.

"Our family will be disgraced." Lord Blackford's voice was low. "Your sister will be touched by your disregard for her and her situation. She will not be able to make as good a match, for no one will want to align themselves with you and Lord Foster, given his utter poverty and foolish character."

"And yet you have not asked her to consider me and my circumstances," Alice retorted, her hands going to her hips as sudden anger flared. "I have never been a consideration of yours, nor of Mama's, nor of my sister's. I shall marry whomever I wish. I shall not be a companion to my aunt, for I wish more than that for myself. I may end up in poverty, but if I do not wed him, then I shall be nothing more than a companion, unable to spend a single moment of my life as my own. Therefore, Father, I will go to Lord Foster, and I will sit with him. And when he suggests a date for our marriage, I shall stand up beside him and take him as my husband, just as you instructed me to do."

So saying, Alice strode from the dining room and made her way directly to the drawing room, where Lord Foster would be waiting. She did not like having to speak so harshly, but she was not about to permit her father to stand between herself and Lord Foster. Whether or not it would disgrace her family, she did not care. The only thing that mattered at present was her situation and her future with Lord Foster. Her anger began to fade as she approached the drawing room. Taking a moment, she settled her hand on the doorknob, drew in a deep breath, closed her eyes, and forced a smile to her lips.

"Lord Foster." Pushing open the door, she stepped inside, closing it behind her when she saw a maid in the corner of the room. "I think you received my note then?"

To her utter surprise, she found herself pulled into Lord Foster's arms at the next moment. His face was in her neck, his hot breath rushing across her skin as she stood there, frozen in place by the whirling emotions that suddenly captured her. There was no anger anymore. There was only shock, astonishment, wonder... and a slow burning desire for more.

"I have been out of my mind with worry." Lord Foster did not let her go. "I thought they had taken you." Another gentle breath seared her skin and Alice closed her eyes. She had never been this close to a gentleman, had never felt such burning emotions sweeping through her, coursing through her veins, demanding every part of her. "When I returned from searching for you, I discovered your note. You cannot know how much relief I felt."

Pulling back just a little, Alice quickly realized that

Lord Foster was wearing the same clothes that she had seen him in last evening.

"You... you have been looking for me all night?"

Lord Foster nodded, the paleness of his face telling her that he spoke the truth.

"I did not hear you leave. When I came out from my hiding place, I thought you would still be there. The fear that took me when I discovered that you were gone...." One hand lifted to cup her face gently. "Forgive me for coming here. I did not know what else to do. I *had* to see your face."

"It is quite all right." Her breathless voice betrayed the swirling desire growing within her. "Only my father is at home, and I believe he is now coming to terms with the fact that his daughter is soon to be wed to a poverty-stricken gentleman." She smiled, trying to make light of the situation so that she would not betray herself. "He will not be able to refuse."

"I feel as though I want to ask you at this very moment whether or not you will marry me." Lord Foster smiled and shook his head, his hand dropping from her cheek. "Are we from this moment betrothed? For my own self, I think it would be best."

Reminding herself that this was nothing but a practical arrangement, Alice smiled at him.

"If you still wish it to be so."

"I wish for nothing else." His gentleness of expression brought her almost to tears and the warmth in his smile sent her heart whirling. The very next moment, however, Lord Foster stepped away, put his hands behind his back and looked away from her. "Then we are betrothed."

"We are."

"Good." Clearing his throat, he turned his head to rest

his gaze on hers. "You say that you have found something important?"

"I... I have." Giving herself a slight shake, Alice opened her mouth to say something more, only for a sudden screech and the slamming of a door to reach them. Lord Foster stepped back again, making certain to put a more than respectful space between them. Alice winced, closing her eyes. "I believe that my mother and sister may have returned, and been informed of our news, Lord Foster." A brief smile touched her mouth, then disappeared again. "Perhaps we might continue this conversation later this evening? I fear that my mother will soon make her presence known to us both, otherwise." Sighing, she tilted her head. "I am to go to the Vauxhall pleasure gardens with my mother and sister this evening. My sister is to be accompanied by Lord Bradford."

"Then I shall find you there."

Lord Foster came close to her again, reaching out one hand. He opened his mouth as if he wanted to say something more, but could not quite find the words to say it. Shaking his head, he cleared his throat, caught her hand, bowed over it rather sharply, and strode from the room. Alice closed her eyes. The sensations that such a small touch had brought to her were overwhelming. Lord Foster had caught her, body and soul, and she had been entirely unprepared for it. A gentle sigh escaped her as she sat down and pushed one hand over her forehead. A weakness in her knees was delightful; the happiness he brought her overwhelming.

"Whatever is the meaning of this?"

At the very next moment, the door was flung open as her mother strode into the room, followed by Henrietta. Her eyes were blazing with fire, her hands akimbo. Henrietta, however, was merely standing to one side, looking at Alice with wide eyes. No doubt their father had informed Henrietta that her sister was betrothed and would soon wed.

"It means that I am betrothed, Mama."

Speaking calmly, Alice rose from her chair.

Her mother threw up her hands.

"You cannot be betrothed. He has not asked for, nor received, your father's consent."

"He does not need to. I told him plainly that my father had made it clear that it was my responsibility to find a suitor. He cannot complain if I have done precisely that!" Spreading her hands, she tried to smile. "I would have thought that you would be pleased. After all, this means that I will not be a burden to you any longer."

"You shall not marry him."

Ignoring her mother's screech, Alice smiled.

"It is already too late. News has already begun to spread around society. I am afraid you must choose your scandal, Mama."

"Choose my scandal?" Lady Blackford snorted indignantly. "Whatever do you mean?"

"I mean to say, Mama, that you must choose between having Lord Foster married to me in a church or through other means. If you should try to stand in the way of my betrothal, I fully intend to stand up with Lord Foster as my husband, one way or another." The strength of her determination sent fire into her heart. "I will become Lady Foster, whether I have to run away with the gentleman, or whether I stand up with him in church. I have chosen my future and I do not intend to allow anyone to take it from me. You must choose which one of those two circumstances you would prefer, for I *will* have him as my husband."

She did not wait for her mother to answer her. Without so much as a glance in her sister's direction, Alice lifted her chin and walked quietly from the room. This was to be her future now, and she would not permit her mother's upset, or her father's anger, to pull it from her.

CHAPTER ELEVEN

"*Y*ou are brooding. Although I suppose, given the circumstances, that is to be expected."

It took William a moment to realize that his friend was speaking to him. Shifting in his chair, he dropped both hands to his lap and shrugged.

"I have much to think about, although I must say I am very glad that you are returned from your estate. Perhaps I ought not to be keeping such thoughts to myself, and instead be sharing them with you."

"If it pertains to our situation at present, then yes. I should be very glad to hear whatever it is you have to say. It has been a difficult time indeed. I was not certain I would even have enough coin to return to London!" Lord Wiltsham shook his head. "I am grateful to you for permitting me to reside in your townhouse for a time."

"I shall soon have to think of what I am to do with it, if I do not recover my fortune." William scowled. "I wish we had never listened to Lord Gillespie, God rest his soul."

"I concur." Lord Wiltsham picked up his glass, which contained a very small measure of brandy since William had very little left, and not the funds to purchase more. "You state that you found something in his study, however. You have not seen it as yet?"

"I have seen it but not read it in its entirety. Miss Lawrence has it, but I fully expect to see it this evening at the Vauxhall Gardens."

Lord Wiltsham's brow lifted.

"And that is what makes you appear so contemplative?"

"In part." Briefly, William explained everything which had taken place. "After Miss Lawrence found the letter from the Viscount, I was so very afraid that she would be gone from me, that something had happened which would remove her from this earth in the same way as Lord Gillespie had been taken. We are now betrothed, I might add."

He threw this remark out casually, but Lord Wiltsham let out such an exclamation of surprise that William jerked visibly.

"You accepted her offer then?"

"I did." William's gaze lingered on his friend as Lord Wiltsham's brows lifted. "We shall marry soon enough - whether or not I regain my fortune, that being said."

Lord Wiltsham said nothing for a few moments, then shrugged.

"I wish you whatever happiness you can find, even though I fear it may be in short supply for some time. But at least you will have someone to share it with, for one thing." His eyes held William's steadily. "Perhaps that is why you are a little more thoughtful at present. You are thinking of the lady."

"I will not pretend that she does not occupy my thoughts and, much to my surprise, I do not find her plain in any way. Rather, I find her character to be one so uncompromisingly beautiful and equally frustrating at the same time. She has a strength about her that I did not initially see. She has a desire for justice not only for herself, but also for my situation. She is trusting. She is filled with hope, and I find myself becoming caught by thoughts of her that will not seem to leave me, no matter what I do."

"Well." Lord Wiltsham picked up his near empty brandy glass. "Then might I wish you happiness? It is a fortunate gentleman who finds himself drawn to the lady he is to wed, even in such strange circumstances as yours!"

William grinned, then took a small sip of his own brandy in a small toast.

"That is indeed true. I was utterly astonished at all that I felt when I thought she had been taken... and then at the relief which sank into my very soul when I realized that she was safe. I have experienced nothing like it. I have found myself wanting to kiss her on more than one occasion, which seems almost ridiculous, given my present circumstances, that I should be thinking of anything other than my fortune! But it is as though she has bewitched me - which is both wonderful and irritating in equal measure."

"I quite understand. I have experienced the touch of love upon my heart, although it appears to be the first time that you have!"

William coughed quietly and shook his head.

"Such emotions are entirely new and confusing to me. I look forward to this evening, not only so that I can see the letter that Miss Lawrence has discovered, as well as hear whatever else it is she wishes to tell me, but also so that I may be in her company once more. Is that not most strange?"

Lord Wiltsham laughed, and suddenly a brightness seemed to fill the room which had not been there before.

"Yes, this is very strange indeed, but I am glad for you.

Let us hope that this letter is what you need, to find the truth - for to regain your fortune and to gain a marriage to a lady whom you have come to care for would be a very pleasant ending indeed."

William grinned.

"I quite agree." Throwing back the rest of his brandy in one rather small gulp, he set down the empty glass on the table. "If I am able to find both success and happiness in this, then it will give you the hope of doing the same, surely. I am certain that you will not find yourself in poverty for the remainder of your days. There is still hope, Wiltsham. Do not allow yourself to drop into despair." He smiled at his friend. "There will be happiness for you also, in time. Just be patient a little longer."

THE EVENING WAS ALREADY dark by the time the *ton* arrived at Vauxhall Gardens. A great many fiery torches were lit, and lanterns brightened the dark evening, although William was glad of the shadows. They hid his face admirably well, and so long as he remained out of doors, the chances were that the *ton*, on the whole, would not notice his presence. Lord Wiltsham had taken some convincing to join him, but at last now they stood together, rather than William finding no company with whom to talk during the entire evening.

"Can you see her yet?"

William shook his head, opening his mouth to say something, just as a loud voice broke into their conversation.

"I hear you have betrothed yourself to my daughter without seeking my consent."

As he turned around to face Lord Blackford, William

caught the glint of steel in the gentleman's eyes which spoke of nothing but anger.

Grimacing, and refusing to be cowed, William held the man's gaze.

"I do believe that you gave your daughter strict instructions that finding a suitor was entirely her responsibility, Lord Blackford." Folding his arms across his chest, he held the man's gaze. "That is what she has done. I do not think that you can find fault with either her or myself."

"And what can you offer her?" Lord Blackford spat, flinging out one hand to tap William's chest. "You have no wealth. You have no fortune, and your character is severely deficient, given that you have lost a good deal of it to a spate of gambling."

"That is not so." William did not look away, nor even blink. "I shall not go into details, but only say that my fortune has been stolen from me. I have every intention of regaining it, but if I do not, then I shall revel in the relief of knowing that I have a woman by my side who believes that everything I say to her is true. We shall struggle through this life together if we must, but together we shall be."

"Then you are inconsiderate and unfeeling. You think only of yourself and not of my daughter. You do not care about her. Keeping her in a crumbling, cold manor house with very little food and very little comfort? Is that what you wish for her and for any children you may force upon her?"

The picture he painted was very bleak indeed, and William's heart dropped to the floor. He had always forced himself to believe that he would regain his fortune and in doing so, had never permitted himself to consider the possibility of a miserable future for himself and Miss Lawrence. Now, he realized, it might well come to pass. If he cared about Miss Lawrence at all, what could he really offer her?

"I believe that your own intentions for your daughter were not so very honorable."

It was Lord Wiltsham's voice which drew William back to the conversation. Lord Blackford made some exclamation of frustration in the man's direction, but it was enough to build William's courage again.

"That is very true." Regaining himself, William lifted his chin. "I believe you were to send her to serve some aunt as her companion, to a situation where she would never wed, where she would never have the possibility of children, or of being mistress of her own home. You cannot say that such a life is the better choice."

Lord Blackford took a step closer.

"Indeed, I can Lord Foster. She is my daughter. *I* am the one who states what her future is to be, not you."

"She is doing precisely as you asked her," William reminded him. "Your daughter knows exactly what her future is to be in either circumstance. Should she not have that choice? I offer her more hope than your future for her ever could."

"Which is precisely why I have accepted him."

A calm clear voice interrupted William's discussion, and he turned just in time to see Miss Lawrence gaze up at her father with stony eyes.

"I cannot permit this." Lord Blackford swiped through the air with his hand, separating William and Miss Lawrence. "You *cannot* marry him. I will not have it."

"I can and I will." Miss Lawrence placed her hand over William's, and he immediately tucked it under his arm. "You cannot deny me, father. You may have forgotten when my birthday is, so let me remind you – I have my majority.

The choice is mine. I have done as you asked, and now you seek to pull me away from the only happiness I might ever have. I *will* marry Lord Foster and I will be happy, whether or not he recovers his fortune."

A gasp came from William's left, and he turned his head to see one of the most prolific gossips in all of London hurrying away from them. He was not angry but rather filled with relief as he settled his gaze upon Lord Blackford once more. The man's eyes were following Lady Greenwood as his shoulders slumped. Evidently, he realized that there was nothing for them to do but accept the situation, as it now stood.

"Should you like to take a turn about the gardens, Miss Lawrence?" With a broad smile, William turned toward his betrothed. "Lord Wiltsham can join us, unless Lord Blackford wishes to be your chaperone?"

Inquiring eyes were met with a blank stare and, with a shrug, William turned away, leading Miss Lawrence away from her father with Lord Wiltsham coming only a few steps behind. They walked on in silence for a few moments until Miss Lawrence began to laugh.

"I am afraid we cannot escape betrothal now, my Lord. If Lady Greenwood has heard of it, then all of London will know of it by the morning."

"I do not find myself concerned in that regard." William smiled at her. "I find myself a little relieved. The worst, it seems, is over. I did not know how your father would react, but at least now there can be no separating us." He pulled her a little closer. "You are tied to me now."

"And I am glad of that."

Miss Lawrence smiled back at him and for a moment, William lost himself in her gaze. It was not until Lord Wiltsham cleared his throat a little distinctly that William recalled the reason he had wanted to speak with her.

"The letter." Taking a deep breath, he set his shoulders, hoping that this would bring him the answer to his struggles. "You found something in the letter?"

"I took the letter with me, Lord Foster."

Pausing in her walk for a moment, Miss Lawrence pulled it out of her pockets and handed it to him.

William's heart quickened as he unfolded it. The dim light made it difficult to read, but he thought he could make out the words, once he drew a little closer to one of the torches, so that he might read it carefully. His eyes ran over the page once, twice, and then he let out a small exclamation of surprise. Miss Lawrence was by his side in a moment.

"What is it?"

Lord Wiltsham was there too, looking over William's shoulder at the paper.

"It seems that Lord Gillespie was a man in great difficulty." Handing the note to his friend, William shook his head. "I had no idea that he was struggling so very much. That note warns Lord Gillespie to do as he has promised, else the money will be taken from his own dwindling coffers. It seems Lord Gillespie had very little choice but to obey what was being demanded of him."

Lord Wiltsham nodded slowly, before returning the note to Miss Lawrence.

"It does give me a trifle more sympathy for the man." Lord Wiltsham shook his head. "The fellow must have been in significant difficulty, and now that I find myself in financial difficulty, I can understand his desperation."

"As can I." William admitted.

"There is no signature." Miss Lawrence handed the

note back to him with a swift shake of her head. "It has Viscount 'M' written upon it, but nothing else."

William's hopes dashed themselves against the rocks at the moment.

"Then I am lost. Just when the clouds began to part, they return to enfold me again. There are *many* Viscounts in London whose title begins with such a letter. Our only course of action is to attempt to distinguish one from the other and thereafter, spend time following each of them in turn to make certain, somehow, that they are, or are not, the gentleman in question." He threw up his hands, knowing he was being ridiculous but at this present moment, he could see no brightness whatsoever. "The note is clear, but it is maddening given that there is no direct path which we are now to take."

"That is not so."

Miss Lawrence's gentle voice was a balm to his fractured soul. Gazing back at her, he held her gaze steadily, seeing the small smile which lifted the corners of her mouth. The hopes which had been splintered slowly began to piece themselves back together as the three began to walk forward once more, not wishing their conversation to be overheard by anyone.

"The reason I disappeared from Lord Gillespie's study was because I followed after the two men who were in the room with us."

William stopped dead, staring back at her with horror crawling across his skin.

"You need not look at me with such shock. It was the only thing I could think to do, for we must know who these men are. It is important for you, is it not? How else are you to discover the reason that they searched through Lord Gillespie's study?"

"That was incredibly dangerous." William did not move, struggling to push away the dread which had torn at him. "The risk you took...."

"I did it for you, Lord Foster."

Miss Lawrence's cheeks flushed as he stepped closer to her, wanting simultaneously to pull her into his arms and berate her for what she had done.

"They could have seen you! Anything could have happened to you."

"But they did not see me." Miss Lawrence brushed her fingers across his cheek. "I did not injure myself. I was not followed. Indeed, I spoke to one of them - he thought me nothing more than a lady of the night and told me to hurry on my way."

William shook his head, no words coming to his lips.

"And what did you learn?" Lord Wiltsham's voice interrupted William's burning thoughts. "Was there anything of importance?"

Miss Lawrence shrugged.

"I cannot yet tell. I know that the gentleman walked into Donley's, the gentleman's club, whilst his man waited outside. He was the one I spoke to. I do not think I have ever seen such a brute of a fellow in a long time! He had more strength in one hand than I have in all of me!"

At that moment, remembered pain hit William in the side of his head as a memory tore through him of the brute who had struck him from behind.

Dropping his head, he ran one hand over his face, just as Miss Lawrence caught his other one, evidently seeing the pain on his face.

"Are you well, Lord Foster?"

William's voice wobbled as he shook his head, hardly

able to believe that she had been standing and talking with the gentleman who had struck him.

"The men in the room, the men that you followed, were those who injured me and stole my fortune. I have recalled that a very strong hand struck me on the side of my head. Whoever stole my fortune clearly had someone on hand to deliver such a blow, and it could only have come from a man with a great deal of strength. And, given that you have seen and spoken to this man, you may now be in danger, Miss Lawrence."

Fear bubbled up in his throat, but immediately, Miss Lawrence grasped his hand and shook her head.

"He will not recognize me. It was very dark, and the man would not be able to recognize my face in broad daylight. I am sure of it. I did nothing more than discover the name of the gentlemen's club in the hope that you might go there and find the name of the man who went in that evening."

Lord Wiltsham caught his breath and William realized at that very same moment exactly what she was suggesting.

"And if a Viscount was there whose title begins with an 'M', then I shall have found the man who has stolen my fortune." Turning to face Miss Lawrence so that he might grasp both of her hands in his, William gazed deeply into her eyes before turning his head away again, not quite certain that he could contain himself if he continued to look at her so. She had done more than speak well of him in society, had done more than he had ever imagined she might be able to do. The courage and fortitude she had shown now led him down a clear path towards victory and restoration - and all because of what she had done. "You are remarkable." William shook his head and closed his eyes, not quite able to find the words to describe everything he felt at this moment. "I should not have berated you for what you did, although my heart still quails at the thought of what could have happened to you. My entire being is singing with joy over with the hope that you have restored to me." Pressing her hands, he moved a little closer to her still. "Only promise me that you shall never do such a thing again."

Miss Lawrence laughed softly and shook her head.

"I am afraid that I cannot give you any such promises, my Lord." Her smile faded a little. "I must pray that this is what you have been seeking. If this is the gentleman who has stolen your fortune, then I beg of you to find a way to make certain of your own safety as you confront him. If he was willing to do such a heinous thing as cheat you out of your fortune, then I am certain he will be willing to do even more. Surely the danger is no longer for me, but for you."

"She is right." Lord Wiltsham glanced at Miss Lawrence and then looked to William. "We must think carefully about how we are to approach this. I am by your side, whether or not you wish me to be," he finished, seeing William's anger burning in his eyes. "Our first endeavors are to be to the gentlemen's club, but thereafter you must give a great deal of consideration as to how you are to proceed. I do not think Miss Lawrence would prefer you gain your fortune only to lose your life."

"No, indeed."

Miss Lawrence's hand caught the top of his arm and William was held fast by the flashes of silver in her beautiful grey eyes. How had he ever thought her plain? To him, she was the most beautiful woman in all of England; her character divine, her gentle nature nothing but sweetness and the beauty of her face capturing his attention with every moment that passed.

"I would rather you were impoverished than dead, Lord

Foster." Miss Lawrence spoke bluntly, her eyes searching his. "Promise me that you will be careful."

"I shall take the utmost care." With Lord Wiltsham fading into the background, he came close to her until his face was only an inch away from her own. "Miss Lawrence, I would express to you just how much my heart feels at this moment. It is not because of what you have done for me, but because of what you have become to me."

Miss Lawrence blinked rapidly, her eyes rounding, but William did not hold himself back. They were betrothed now, so he could speak openly and earnestly without fear that she would run from him.

"I am as astonished as you appear to be, but let me speak the truth. There is more in my heart for you, Miss Lawrence, than mere friendship. There is so much more to learn and to say, I am sure, but for the moment let me express to you just how much I admire you, how much I owe you and how grateful I am for you."

A loud giggle from a lady walking arm in arm with her friend stole the moment. Miss Lawrence dropped her head and Lord Wiltsham cleared his throat, leaving William a little frustrated. Letting out a breath, he set his shoulders and stepped back.

"Come, let us walk together a little more before I return you to your mother."

Over his shoulder, he saw Lord Wiltsham nod in answer to William's silent question. After their turn about the grounds, William had every intention of making directly to Donley's and seeking the name of the gentleman who had been there only the previous evening. The gentleman who might hold the answers to all of his questions. The gentleman who had ruined his life.

~

"I MUST SEE YOUR BOOK."

The man stepped back for a moment in surprise at William's request, but William held his ground, looking at him steadily as if he fully expected him to obey without question.

"Are you a patron here, my Lord?"

The man was short but stocky, with a tightness about his expression, appearing to be a little more defiant than William had expected.

"I am not." Speaking honestly, William shrugged. "But I must see your ledger nonetheless."

The man shook his head.

"I am sorry."

William glanced towards Lord Wiltsham. He had to find a way to see the ledger, but he was not certain what to say which would allow him access. There was, of course, the choice to take the ledger by force if it was required, but he would rather not do so.

Lord Wiltsham's lips quirked.

"Come here a moment, my good fellow." Lord Wiltsham cocked his head to the left and, after a moment of doubt, the fellow stepped nearer. From where William stood, he could hear Lord Wiltsham's low tones and saw how he stooped just a little, as if to make out that there was some very great secret to be whispered in the man's ear.

"We come on the King's business."

A flash of shock rushed through William, but he held himself tightly, making sure to nod when the little man looked at him.

"It is not something that we wished to tell you. It is a matter of great delicacy. The gentleman we seek is of interest to the King, but as yet he cannot make this known to anyone, for fear that society will hear of it. My friend here was not certain you could keep such a secret, but perhaps he was mistaken in that regard. After all, you appear to be most intelligent, eager to make certain that all propriety is followed."

The man's gaze traveled towards William, and William spread his hands.

"I am sorry. I have no intention of insulting you in any way, but you must understand that the King's business can only be undertaken in the greatest secrecy. You are not known to me, and I am not known to you. Therefore, I thought it best to remain steadfastly silent."

"I quite understand." A thin-lipped smile crossed the man's face. "I can be trusted. I keep a great many secrets, as is required of me in my profession. The King can trust me."

"I am sure he will be most grateful. Might we now look at your ledger?"

Lord Wiltsham gave the man a small smile as William's breath tightened in his chest. The small man considered for a moment longer, tilting his head just a little.

"But of course, anything for the King."

Without further complaint, the small man returned to his desk, picked up the ledger from behind it and handed it directly to Lord Wiltsham, rather than to William as though he had taken personal insult over William's lack of trust in him. Lord Wiltsham studied it for a few moments, then passed it to William.

William did not hesitate. Searching avidly with his eyes, he ran his gaze down the ledger, searching desperately for the one name which would answer all of his prayers. There had been quite a few patrons the previous evening, and for a few seconds, William was afraid that he would not find the gentleman in question.

And then, he found it – the name which had to be the one he sought.

Running his fingers over it, William narrowed his eyes, hurriedly searching the rest of the page for any other gentleman who had a title that began with the same letter.

There were none.

His heart leaped in his chest as he snapped the ledger shut before looking toward Lord Wiltsham. His friend gave him a small nod.

"Thank you. We have found what we are looking for." William gave the small man a brief smile. "I will make sure to tell the King of your willingness in this. I am certain that he will offer a few words about this establishment to his many friends and acquaintances."

The man's eyes flared.

"But of course. I would do anything for His Majesty." He bowed low, as though he were acknowledging the King himself. "I am only glad that I could be of assistance."

William and Lord Wiltsham did not waste another moment, turning on their heels as they marched sharply out of Donley's and into the fresh air. The night was dark, and nobody saw them emerge. William stopped short, his breathing coming in ragged gasps as he put his hands on his knees and bent forward, hardly able to take in that he now had the name of someone connected to the loss of his fortune.

"I believe that we have a great deal to thank Miss Lawrence for," Lord Wiltsham murmured, putting one hand on William's shoulder. "I am glad for you. I hope that you can find this Lord Montague."

William nodded, pushing himself up to standing.

"I am certain I will be able to do so. A quick word to one of my servants will soon have the answers I seek. I am more than grateful that I have been able to retain a few of them!"

A wry smile tipped Lord Wiltsham's lips, but it was gone the next second.

"And what shall you do once you face him?"

A cloud covered the moon and William could not see his friend's expression in the dim light.

"I do not yet know."

He realized that he had spent so long thinking about how to discover exactly who was responsible that he had not given much thought to what he would do thereafter.

"It will come to you once you have given it a little more thought. You will keep me informed?"

"I certainly shall." William sighed and waved one hand towards the empty street. "I must walk back to my town-house, for I cannot afford the carriage. I have not enough servants to use it!"

"With that, I can sympathize." Lord Wiltsham chuckled. "We will walk together and keep each other from being a victim of some street thieves. I look forward to your ideas on when and where you intend to deal with Lord Montague."

William's heart grew suddenly heavy.

"Thank you, my friend. I look forward to the moment when I will finally regain what is mine."

CHAPTER TWELVE

"It is Lord Montague."

Alice caught her breath as Lord Foster came close to her, his breath tickling her cheek, his hand on her shoulders, smoothing down her arm until his fingers caught hers.

"You are quite sure?"

"Entirely so. And it is thanks to you that I have such confidence. The name of the gentleman on the ledger was Viscount Montague, which in turn fits with the letter we retrieved from Lord Gillespie's study. I confess that I am not as angry with Lord Gillespie's behavior any longer, God rest him. I realize the difficult situation he was in, struggling with his coffers and seeing no way to remove himself from the noose that such men as Lord Montague had tied around his neck. He chose to obey and, in doing so, quite ruined me and my friends - but perhaps he felt as though he had very little choice." Alice swallowed hard, trying to concentrate on what he was saying, but her emotions continued to muddle her mind. She wanted to linger, wanted to put her hands around his neck and draw his head down towards hers. "Miss Lawrence?"

She jumped, her skin prickling.

"Yes, I quite agree." *I must concentrate on what he is saying rather than on what I am feeling.* "What is it that you intend to do?"

"I intend to speak to the man directly." Anger flashed across his face, darkening his green eyes. "I have spent an entire evening thinking about what it is I am to do, and I believe that I have found a way to force Lord Montague's hand. I am quite certain that he will not return my fortune without force."

Alice sucked in a breath, and before she knew it, she found her hands clinging to him. One was coiled in his shirt, ruining its perfect appearance completely, and the other was at his shoulder, pulling at his jacket. Fear was scrabbling at her and, despite her best attempt to contain it, threatened to take a stronger hold.

"But you will not... *cannot* use force against him! He is a man willing to do whatever he must to gain whatever he wants. If you attempt to use your own strength against him, I fear that he will return in such a manner also. He may well have been responsible for Lord Gillespie's death. He has already injured you to the point of unconsciousness. What if he does more? I cannot lose you."

To her surprise, Lord Foster caught her fingers. Alice made to drop both of her hands, embarrassed to have behaved so, but Lord Foster only clung to them.

"Do you truly care for me so deeply?"

The anger had faded from his eyes, and there was a soft smile on his mouth. Licking her lips, Alice fought for an answer, darting her gaze to one side, afraid of what he would see in her eyes. If she were honest, she would state that she felt a great deal for Lord Foster - more than she had ever expected, for in their coming together, she had realized just how much of a gentleman he truly was. He was not foolish nor greedy, as the *ton* thought. Instead, he was nothing but kindness and consideration. The fierceness with which he pursued the truth won her admiration. The way he had trusted her heart and trusted her to keep her promises had built up the strength of feeling between them.

"I cannot pretend that I do not care for you a little, Lord Foster." Trying to keep her voice light, Alice shot him a smile but kept her eyes away. "Even if we end up as paupers, I shall always be happy with my choice."

Lord Foster's thumb ran back and forward over her hand, building waves of heat that seemed to flow ever faster as she struggled to know what to say next. A daring glance in his direction showed that he was smiling tenderly at her. She had no need to be embarrassed by her emotions, she realized. Was there even a flicker of happiness in his eyes? Was there anything that he would offer her in return?

"I do not think I deserve you."

"Nonsense." Waving her free hand, she tried to smile. Her emotions were building so quickly that if they did not begin to talk of something else, she might find herself saying things that would not be wise to speak of at the present moment. "Tell me when you are to speak to Lord Montague. I shall go with you, of course."

That shattered the stillness between them, for Lord Foster immediately began to protest, but Alice ignored his concerns. She was not about to permit him to refuse her.

"Lord Montague is not a man to be trifled with, as you have said yourself, I cannot permit you to be in danger."

"He has all the more reason to behave a little more carefully if a woman is present," she reminded him. "Please. I must hear Lord Montague's defense for what he has done. The *ton* shall have to know of what takes place, and I can only speak of what I have seen." Lord Foster shook his head. "Please." Putting her free hand over their joined ones, she looked earnestly into his face. "We have been together all through this, have we not? Let us be together until the very end of the matter. I am not afraid, despite the danger. I must be there in support of you. Not only because I care for you, but also because I am angry about what this gentleman has done to you. Allow me to stand to one side - behind the door if it is required - but please, Lord Foster. Allow me to be present."

Lord Foster searched her eyes, dropped his head, and then let out a small sigh.

"I believe you could ask me anything and I would not refuse you, Miss Lawrence."

His eyes caught hers again, and Alice's heart beat with a wild hope.

"Then you will allow me to be there when you speak to Lord Montague?"

"Yes, I shall. I could not do anything but oblige you, despite my misgivings. You shall remain silent, however, and out of sight. Those are my requirements. I do not wish you to draw attention to yourself for your safety." His smile was tight. "I cannot say what Lord Montague will do."

There was no reason for her to refuse his request.

"Of course, my Lord, but I cannot state that I will remain entirely silent for, if Lord Montague should think of stepping forward to engage you in anything... physical, then I would find myself eager to do what I could."

It seemed that Lord Foster was not about to permit her to even *think* of doing such a thing, however. He shook his head firmly, moving even closer still so that there was barely an inch between them.

"You must do nothing of the sort. If there is to be any altercation, then I must beg of you to stay far from it, for that is the only way that I can protect you. Besides which, I shall have Lord Wiltsham with me also." His fingers threaded through hers. "I could not live if you were to come to harm. Promise me, my dear, that you will not come near Lord Montague, no matter what he does or what he says."

Alice wanted to refuse, wanted to tell him that she could not stay away should the worst happen, but at the same time, she saw the desperation in his eyes.

"No matter what happens, I will not reveal myself to Montague," she promised, her voice soft.

"Do you swear it?"

His face was so close to her that his breath was catching her lips, almost drawing her to him. Her eyes flickered closed as she took in a shaking breath. Had they not been very much hidden by one of the large pillars in Almack's and by the shadows of the room, she might well have reconsidered her nearness to him, but as it stood, she could not help but stay close to him.

"I swear it."

There was the briefest touch of his lips against her own. Alice caught her breath, desperate for him to linger, desperate for him to pull her into his arms so that she could be his, body and soul, but emptiness appeared where he had been. The warmth of his body was gone, his breath only a distant memory. Opening her eyes, Alice found herself quite alone, her eyes fixed on the retreating back of Lord Foster.

∽

"You remember your promise."

"I do." Alice gripped her reticule tightly with both hands. "And I have every intention of keeping it."

Lord Foster smiled, but it did not bring even the slightest spark to his eyes.

"Thank you. That is a relief to me. Lord Montague is expecting a gentleman by the name of Lord Peters, a gentleman he is well acquainted with. Of course, it is not Lord Peters who will be attending him, but myself and Lord Wiltsham. There will be no opportunity for him to escape our presence." Taking a deep breath, Lord Foster turned to face her, instead of looking towards the door. Lightning bolts were in his eyes; he was somewhere between anger and fervent hope. "I must go in. The door will be ajar. You may listen to everything that is said, but I beg of you, my dear Alice, *please* stay out of sight. It is for your safety that I say such a thing with such fervency."

Alice could only nod. Her heart was already beating furiously, and she was suddenly afraid of what would happen to the man she had come to care so much about. Lord Montague might not just take away Lord Foster's fortunes this time, he might take away his life. The fleeting kiss they had shared flashed through her memory, and before she knew what she was doing, Alice found herself standing on tiptoe, her mouth pressed to Lord Foster's. It was a desperate, beautiful, overwhelming moment, for in that kiss there was all the hope for her future and all the fear of what could happen next.

Lord Foster's mouth was soft beneath hers. His arms went around her waist, and he held her close, not pulling her tight against him, but the gentle embrace seemed to take all of her fear and tug it away from her so that he might carry it himself. When he broke the embrace, his thumb ran across her cheek, and he smiled down into her eyes.

"You have given me this, Alice. You have given me *all* of this. Whether or not I am successful, I shall be forever grateful for what we now share. In a strange way, I do not think it would have taken place had I not lost everything in this manner. I think you can tell that I find myself bound to you. Our marriage, whether in poverty or in wealth, will be a happy one, I am sure."

Alice tried to find something to say. Her lips parted, but no words came out. The next moment he was gone, leaving her standing there alone as tears pricked in the corners of her eyes. Blinking furiously, not wanting a single one to drop to her cheeks, she whispered aloud to herself.

"All will be well. I must believe that all will be well."

It did not take long for the conversation between Lord Montague, Lord Foster, and Lord Wiltsham to begin. Alice remained hidden behind the door. It was half closed but left ajar so that she might hear what was being said. Lord Foster had arranged this meeting, pretending to be an acquaintance of Lord Montague's, and begging him for a private audience in one of the smaller rooms at Almack's. Lord Montague had not appeared to take much convincing, evidently believing that this was, in fact, his old friend. Of the large, broad-shouldered man, Alice could not yet see or hear anything. Perhaps, if they were lucky, he would not make an appearance. She only hoped that would be the case.

"I do not believe that we have met. You are not Lord Peters." Lord Montague's voice was low and filled with an anger even Alice could hear. "You have brought me here under false pretenses."

"Much like I was brought to the copper hells in East London under false pretenses." Lord Foster's voice was clear. "You need not pretend. I am well aware of who you are, Lord Montague. You held Lord Gillespie's fate in your hands, and you used his situation to your own advantage, did you not?"

There came a couple of seconds of silence before Lord Montague began to laugh. Alice closed her eyes and shuddered a little, afraid that the man was about to deny everything, but in the next moment that fear blew itself out.

"I shall not pretend to be anything other than what you have laid before me." Lord Montague's voice was cheerful, as if he were glad that Lord Foster had discovered him. "It is as you say. Alas, your fortune was given to me, and I can do nothing other than continue to use it as I see fit. After all, the wager was lost."

The mockery in his tone made Alice's skin crawl and despite her fear, her hands curled into tight fists.

"That is not the truth. I was tricked into that game. I have no recollection of signing any documents or of promising you my fortune. Whatever it was that you placed in my drink that evening had the desired effect."

Again, the man's voice filled the room with laughter. Quite how Lord Foster withstood it, Alice did not know. She wanted to burst into the room, stride towards Lord Montague and demand that he return Lord Foster's fortune without delay, but her promise to Lord Foster lingered in her mind and she knew she could not.

"Is that so?"

"It is." Lord Foster's voice had risen with anger. "Lord

Gillespie was the one who sent my friends and I there, but it was at your behest, was it not?"

There was a breath of silence.

"I will not be pushed into details, but nor will I take the entirety of your supposed blame. Many gentlemen play at those copper hells. You cannot truly think that there was any *deliberate* action involved in you sitting at the same table as I."

"That is precisely what I think."

Another curl of laughter came from Lord Montague and Alice drew back from the door as his voice came nearer.

"You are a fool. You can gain nothing from this. I may as well be on my way, for there is very little point in this discussion. You shall not take your fortune back from me. It was given to me in all truth, and you shall not have it."

Alice closed her eyes and breathed deeply, pushing down the panic which swirled in her belly. Was Lord Montague about to leave? It seemed as though Lord Foster's ventures were quite lost. Yes, he had found the culprit, but there did not appear to be anything that could be done to force Lord Montague's hand.

"That is where you are a little mistaken." Much to Alice's surprise, there was a confidence in Lord Foster's voice, a confidence she had not expected. "I did not think that any sort of discussion would convince you to return what is mine, what was stolen from me. I did not expect you to be a gentleman with any scruples. Therefore, I thought to do much as you did to me."

There was a short silence.

"What do you mean?"

The man had not yet left the room and, to Alice's delight, there was a faint hint of concern in Lord

Montague's voice. He no longer sounded as confident as she had heard him be at first.

"Your brandy did not taste a little strange, I hope."

A darkness flitted in and out of Lord Foster's voice.

"You can do nothing." Lord Foster's words did not appear to have had any effect on Lord Montague, who continued arrogantly. "Even if I am a little overtaken by whatever you have placed in my brandy, I shall not give you what you want. I have enough strength of mind for that. And bear in mind, Lord Foster, I know *exactly* what it is you have planned. You, however, were much more easily led than I shall ever be. In a way, I pity your weakness."

Alice's fingernails bit into the soft skin of her palms as she fought back the anger which built in her chest. A door opened a little further down the hallway, and as Alice stared at the approaching figure, she realized with horror that it was none other than the broad-shouldered fellow who had been with Lord Montague in the days before. To her mind, it now appeared as though Lord Foster had no other option but to give up. If this man made his way into the room, then he would do precisely as Lord Montague bade him, and Lord Foster would no doubt find himself grievously injured.

I would rather live in poverty than see him so injured.

Taking a step forward, Alice lifted her chin and stood directly in his path. To her surprise, he lifted an eyebrow inquiringly, stopped, and crossed his arms while still gazing at her. He did not appear to want to enter. Perhaps he was waiting for his master to call him in.

I promised Lord Foster that I would not go into the room. That does not mean that I cannot do something here.

"You must not go in."

Taking a step closer, Alice folded her arms across her chest, copying the stance of the man in front of her.

"I am afraid that I must." The man tilted his head, studying her. "It appears you are not a lady of the night as I had first thought. What are you, then?"

"I am a friend. I come only to support my... friend, who has been poorly treated indeed. And it is your master who has done it."

A flicker of a frown pulled at the man's forehead.

"Is that so?" Even still, he did not move. "And yet, I must enter the room when I am called. It is my duty."

Alice shook her head.

"No." She was well aware of how ridiculous she sounded, given that she was so slight compared to this fellow, but her determination could match his. "I cannot allow you entry."

A chuckle made her skin crawl.

"I am afraid you will be entirely unable to stop me." The man's voice had become a little harder. "I have no wish to injure you, for you have no place in this. But if I must, I will remove you by force."

Alice trembled outwardly, but kept her eyes fixed on his. She was no match for his physical strength, but her determination was greater, she told herself.

"I shall do everything I can to prevent you. Perhaps it will be enough to hold you back for only a few short moments, but those moments will be enough to ensure that Lord Foster is quite safe."

Her words were short and tight, building a fire of twisted anger which was swiftly followed by a cooling fear when the large man stepped closer. Alice knew that she had no chance of preventing him from entering the room, but she told herself that she did not need to do exactly that. All she needed to do was make certain that he was delayed in the hope that it would give Lord Foster the very best opportunity to make his escape.

The hum of voices from the room continued, and Alice realized that she had not followed the conversation for some minutes. Lord Montague was still laughing, but mocking Lord Foster and Lord Wiltsham. He had already admitted that he had taken Lord Foster's fortune, but as yet he had offered no explanation as to how he was to return it.

"You are a fool, Foster." Lord Montague's laugh bit through Alice's fear. "Do you think Lord Gillespie's defiance was enough to stop me? Do you not realize that I have enough wealth and connections to order someone to do whatever I wish, no matter how dark or cruel it may appear?"

Alice caught her breath, her hand rising to her mouth as she forgot about the broad-shouldered man standing there. It now appeared that Lord Montague had paid someone to kill Lord Gillespie, all because the man had tried to bring the whole scheme to an end. Nausea rolled through her stomach, and she squeezed her eyes closed.

"There's nothing in this brandy." Lord Montague spat out one word after another. "Whatever you planned to do, you have failed spectacularly. Why do you not leave here and try to make the best of the situation? You shall have no sympathy from me."

"You killed Lord Gillespie."

"I did not do so personally." Lord Montague's voice was shrill. "I required his willingness – we all did – and he was no longer willing to give it. I believe he had every intention of telling you and your friends exactly what had happened, and I could not allow that. And nor do I regret ordering it."

"You are wickedness itself."

Lord Wiltsham spoke words that Alice could not help but agree with.

"And you *shall* return my fortune and this scheme of yours will come to an end," Lord Foster added as the broad-shouldered man stepped forward. "I have made certain that you cannot refuse."

Again came Lord Montague's harsh laugh and to Alice's horror, she saw the broad-shouldered man with one hand outstretched towards the door. Terror coiled in her belly, but she used it to drive herself forward, pushing him back with both hands. The next second, however, she was lifted bodily off her feet and set to one side. The man growled at her as he returned to the door, and Alice only had a few moments to center herself again. She rushed at him again, her fears building, but the man put out one hand towards her. As she practically fell into it, he pushed her back with ease. Stumbling, she did not quite fall to the floor, but took some time to regain her balance, by which time the man had walked into the room.

"No!"

With fear still pushing her every move, Alice found herself rushing into the room after the fellow. She had no idea what she was to do, grabbing wildly at him, but he swatted her back as though she were nothing more than a fly.

"Is this your plan?" Lord Montague threw out one hand towards Alice. "A young lady?" His laugh rang around the room, and Alice closed her eyes, taking in gasping breaths. "I'm afraid that I will not be turned aside from my intentions by a chit, of all things. David here will make sure that I can leave these premises without difficulty and, perhaps, Lord Foster, he will teach you a lesson so that you do not come near me again."

Alice tried to say something, but all that came out was a choking sob as David approached Lord Foster. The gentleman did not shrink back, as though waiting for the blow which would rob him of his strength without fear. He held David's gaze and Alice cried out, suddenly afraid that she would lose Lord Foster forever. Could a blow from this man's hand do more than render a fellow unconscious?

"I do not think you understand me, Lord Montague."

To Alice's utter shock, David turned suddenly, standing next to Lord Foster as he folded his arms and looked towards Lord Montague instead. Lord Wiltsham was smiling, but Alice still did not understand.

"It seems that you have not been treating David particularly well, Montague." Lord Foster lifted one eyebrow. "You have not paid his wages in three months and yet expect him to be at your call whenever you wish it! I do not think that particularly fair."

"That is not true." Lord Montague immediately began to stutter, his face a little pale. "It cannot be three months. I am sure that..."

David took two steps closer to Lord Montague and immediately the gentlemen's excuses dried up, as Montague realized that the strength he had once used against others was now a threat to himself. It seemed that even he was afraid of what David might do.

"It has been *over* three months." David's angry words rattled around the room. "Whenever I dared complain, you threatened my family. My *mother*."

"And," Lord Foster continued, "you have withheld food on occasion, knowing that he has very little coin of his own. Did you expect such behavior to make David more amenable to you? I can assure you that your actions have just done the very opposite." Strolling forward, he slapped one hand on the man's shoulder. "David has told me everything. I am well aware of your schemes, and *he* will be the one to accompany you to your solicitors, where you will return my fortune to me."

Lord Montague immediately began to splutter.

"You cannot do such a thing!"

His eyes were wild, darting around the room as if trying to find some way to escape. There was no bravado now.

"Can I not?" Lord Foster lifted an eyebrow. "I think you will find that I will do a great many things if I have to."

Lord Montague shook his head, planted both hands on his hips and lifted his head.

"I shall not do it. You may use as much strength as you like, but I shall not give you back your fortune. You cannot demand it of me. You cannot force me. David may injure me so severely that I find myself without any strength whatsoever, but I still shall not sign your fortune back to you."

There was a slight tremble to his voice, but his words were determined.

Alice's heart sank. She did not much like the use of violence, but in this circumstance, that seemed to be the only threat that Lord Montague might have responded to. Now it seemed that even that was not going to work.

"I did not suggest that David would use force. Not physical force, at least."

As Alice watched, Lord Foster meandered his way towards Lord Montague, closing the distance between them. His posture was relaxed, and he appeared to be very calm indeed. There was more to this plan of his, Alice realized. She ought not to have doubted for a second.

"Then you admit you have no sway here?" Lord Montague laughed, trying to regain his cocky demeanor. "You can do nothing."

Lord Foster spread out both hands wide.

"Given that David has been your manservant, might you take a moment to consider just how much he knows about you and all of your undertakings?"

All the air left the room. There was clearly a great threat in such words, for Lord Montague's smile fixed itself in place as his eyes widened. Alice had very little idea as to what a gentleman such as Lord Montague might spend his time doing, but she considered that it would not be in any way proper nor upright.

"And what if such news spread through London? What would happen then?" Lord Foster dropped his hands to his side. "A gentleman would face more than one duel; do you not think? And there is no promise that he would always be the crack shot. There would be the chance of him losing his life in one such match."

"I suppose that would depend on how good a shot he is."

Lord Wiltsham, who had remained mostly silent up until this point, crossed both arms and shrugged, keeping his eyes pinned to Lord Montague. Alice looked from one gentleman to the next, finally returning her gaze to Lord Montague. He was paler than she had ever seen him, staring at Lord Foster as if he had not realized just how much strength was in the gentleman's character. Lord Foster was standing quietly, tilting his head to one side as he waited for Lord Montague's reply.

It came soon after.

"I shall return your fortune to you at once." The man was spluttering again. "At this very moment, in fact. David, come."

He turned, but the broad-shouldered man did not follow.

"David is no longer in your employ. He is in mine." Lord Foster smiled, and David flashed a quick grin back in return. "Assured that I would regain my fortune, he will have a better wage and better circumstances than if he remained with you. Listen to me closely, Lord Montague: you will return every single coin to me. Everything that you do between this moment and the return of my fortune will be carefully watched, and if there is even a single thing that is questionable, then some of your darkest secrets will be revealed to the biggest gossips amongst the *ton*."

Lord Montague was a different character from the man who had stood there only a few minutes ago. His head dropped, his shoulders hunched, and he nodded, realizing that he had no other option but to agree. There came no words of rebuttal, no choking laugh which took the whole room in its power. Instead, he was a shadow of who he had been, broken by Lord Foster's wisdom and determination.

Alice had never felt as much relief as in this moment. Her heart ached to be close to Lord Foster again, to rest her head upon his shoulder, to put her arms around his neck so that he might hold her tight to him, but instead she remained precisely where she was, watching as Lord Montague left the room.

Lord Foster had won.

~

"I DID THINK that I asked you to remain behind the door."

Alice stepped forward, only now becoming aware of how much her legs were trembling.

"I did try, she admitted, "but when I saw David approaching, I had to do something." When the man in question glanced at her, Alice gave him a quick smile, aware of the mounting heat in her face. "I am sorry. I did not realize that he was working with you, Lord Foster, not against you."

"I did not tell anyone. The truth was that I was a little uncertain as to whether David was going to accept my offer. I am very glad to see that he did, however. Turning, he held out one hand towards David, who immediately grasped it. Alice sighed happily as the two men shook hands.

"I should follow Lord Montague. Excuse me."

David retired from the room, his long strides eating up the ground. No doubt he would be by Lord Montague's side in only a few moments.

Lord Wiltsham came over to them, putting one hand on each of their shoulders. A broad grin tugged at his lips, as though he were the one who had found his fortune again.

"You have given us all hope." He patted Lord Foster's arm. "I admit that I was lost in a great deal of doubt and uncertainty at one time, and did not believe that there would be even the smallest hope for us. But now I see that it can be done! It is possible to regain one's fortune."

"Yes, I believe that it is possible – for all of us." Lord Foster looked back towards Alice, then let his gaze travel towards his friend again, smiling in a way that Alice had never seen before. It was as though he were free again, free to live as he pleased without any great cloud of doubt or misunderstanding hanging over his head. "I was right, was I not?" There was no boastfulness in his words, but rather a quiet confidence as he spoke to Lord Wiltsham. "We were cheated of our fortunes; they were not taken from us by our own actions. If I was cheated of mine, then you were most certainly cheated of yours. I must tell the others also, so that they can have the confidence to search for those responsible. There are more men than Lord Montague working in this scheme – and if our friends find them, then happiness such as this can be theirs also." Lord Wiltsham nodded, but Alice noticed that there was no smile drawing itself across his lips any longer. Her heart ached for him. She could not imagine what it must be like to see a friend's fortune restored and be glad of it, but at the same time struggle with one's own circumstances which remained entirely the same. "And you shall not struggle any longer. I will rehire your servants. You will have your carriage and your horses and remain in London to live just as you please. I will give you everything that you need."

Lord Wiltsham immediately shook his head.

"No, you cannot. You have your own fortune, and I shall regain mine in time."

"Do you really think I would allow you to continue living in poverty whilst I am reveling in my good fortune?" Lord Foster's voice was warm. "You have stood by me in this. You have been beside me and aided me in my search, and I must repay that. Consider it a loan if you must, but I will give you the money that you require to restore you to your previous situation. I am going to insist on this, Wiltsham. You can say nothing to dissuade me."

Alice smiled softly as Lord Wiltsham's head dropped forward. He did not look at either of them, but his shoulders were rounding in such a way that Alice knew he was battling with his emotions.

"I thank you." His voice was thin. "I shall not refuse your offer. You cannot know how grateful I am to you, Foster. I will be able to hire a valet again!"

Lord Foster chuckled.

"But of course, old friend. We could not have your butler continuing to dress you now, could we?" Laughing, he slapped his friend's shoulder again and then dropped his hand. "With David beside him, I highly doubt that Lord Montague will have any chance to deviate from what he has been directed to do." Turning to Alice, he offered her his arm. "Come, my dear Alice, let us go, so that you might see your betrothed's fortune restored." He leaned towards her, dropping his voice low. "And we shall have to talk about your endeavors this afternoon at another time, so that I might reprimand you for your determination and yet be glad of it at the same time."

Laughing softly, Alice took his arm.

"You may do as you wish, my Lord," she replied, a teasing note in her voice. "But I shall not regret my actions today. I cannot tell you how glad I am that all of this has come to pass, without difficulty or injury. Although," she continued, dropping her voice low as Lord Wiltsham quickened his steps out of the room ahead of them. "You must know that I would have wed you whether or not you had your fortune. The only thing I wanted was for you to be kept quite safe from Lord Montague's darkness."

"I am well aware of that." Stopping briefly, he dropped his head and brushed his lips over hers. "I count myself more blessed than any gentleman in England - not because I have regained my fortune, but because I have such a jewel as you by my side."

His compliments made her cheeks burn, but her heart soar. She wanted to say more, but in the next moment, Lord Foster drew her from the room and they made their way outside. It was time for all things to be restored.

CHAPTER THIRTEEN

inishing his final letter, William set down his quill with a sigh. He had written to the four other gentlemen who had returned to their estates, telling them all that had happened, in the hope that they would find some encouragement from his circumstances. There would be some, whether rightly or wrongly, who would blame themselves for what had happened. They would tell themselves repeatedly that it was now their burden to bear, given that it had been their foolish choices that had forced such a situation upon them. William was desirous to make certain that they did not continue to believe that, and instead see that there was hope. Hope that they could recover what was taken from them. It would take a great deal of effort and certainly a good deal of courage, given that there was no promise of success, but he had to show them that possibility. He had seen the change in Lord Wiltsham's demeanor when the fellow had seen William's success and wanted very much to offer that same encouragement to the rest of his friends.

He rose from his chair and went to ring the bell, smiling

to himself at the indulgence of being able to do so, and in the confidence that the servant would soon appear to take his letters from him. It had only been for a short while that he had lived without such things, but to have them restored made him all the more grateful for what he now had.

A tap at the door indicated that a footman had arrived, and William called for him to enter before handing him the letters. The footman nodded.

"You have two invitations also, my Lord. I will bring them directly."

William continued smiling to himself as the footman hurried from the room. It was amazing how quickly he had recovered himself, now that his fortune was once again his. Society, on the other hand, as Alice had predicted, had not been so easily forgiving, clearly wondering how William had managed to build his fortune again. They would not listen to his explanation. They had no eagerness to do so, for their only intention was to whisper about him and to come up with as many stories as they could. These two invitations would be solely to encourage his presence so that the *ton*'s interest would be piqued.

William did not care. He did not require society's blessing nor their approval. All that he needed was Alice, and her promise to commit herself to him for the rest of her days. The wedding could not come quickly enough.

Another tap came at the door, and William called for the footman to enter, expecting invitations. Instead, the man approached with a silver tray in his hand and a calling card upon it.

"My Lord, you have a visitor. The butler has placed him in the drawing room at present."

Taking the card, William looked down at it, only for his brows to lift in astonishment and his heart to quicken.

Why was it that Lord Blackford had come to call upon him? What could be the purpose of his visit? They had said nothing to each other since the night at the Vauxhall Gardens. Perhaps, in light of William's restored fortune, he now came in an attempt to make amends. William bit his lip. Would he be willing to try and make amends for Alice's sake? Rising to his feet, William gestured to his desk.

"I will return to this presently."

The footman nodded, and William strode from the room. There was a great deal in his heart when it came to Lord Blackford. He did not much like the man, given how he had treated his eldest daughter, and had no willingness to engage him in conversation. Nor had he any urgency to let him explain himself. As far as William was concerned, anything he said about Alice would be nothing other than an excuse, and William was not inclined to listen to excuses.

"Lord Blackford."

Sweeping into the drawing room, William did not so much as bow and Lord Blackford did not rise from his seat. Tension crackled, heating the air. Taking his seat, William sat near the edge, keeping his back straight. He did not want to give any appearance of weakness.

"I hear that you have regained your fortune." Lord Blackford's voice was quiet. "Is that so?"

"It is."

Keeping his eyes on the older gentleman, William did not say anything more.

"There are varying supposed explanations as to how you have regained it."

A twisted smile told William that the gentleman had no particular interest in hearing the truth.

"I am sure that many have come up with an explanation

which suits them. That does not mean that any of them are correct."

Lord Blackford's eyes glinted.

"They say that you have stolen it."

William let out a short huff of breath.

"Why do you not tell me the truth about your reasons for calling upon me this afternoon? Yes, I have regained my fortune. I am due to wed your daughter. What else is there for us to discuss? I have no time to speak of rumors."

Lord Blackford sat back in his chair, his hands on the arms and his head a little tipped to one side, studying William with narrowed eyes, as if he were trying to work out just how formidable an opponent William was to be.

"I want you to remove yourself from my daughter."

William shook his head.

"No."

"There is no reason for you to continue to tie yourself to her." Lord Blackford's voice was hard. "You have regained your fortune. You have no need of a match with her. Let things be as they were before, she will go to her aunt, as has long been suggested, and you may marry anyone you wish."

A smile spread across his thin lips, sending a rush of pain straight through William's heart. This man cared nothing for his daughter. Not a single ounce of consideration went towards her.

"No."

"I do not think you truly understand!" Lord Blackford spread his hands as though William was being unreasonable. "There is no need for my daughter to linger in London any longer. My sister has long been expecting her arrival and we have no one else as a companion for her save for Alice. If you have your fortunes restored to you, then why should you need to continue this betrothal? Any gentleman's daughter is now available to you. Why should you tie yourself to someone as plain and as ordinary as my eldest daughter?"

William's stomach was roiling at the cruelty and inconsideration expressed by Lord Blackford. How had Alice endured this? How had she managed to continue with such pain? His heart twisted in agony for her and yet, with that, came the silent promise that he would not allow such things to continue.

"You could offer me anything, Lord Blackford, and I would refuse it. I would refuse it wholeheartedly." Speaking quietly, he let anger mount itself into his words. "Do you think that I am as cruel and as unfeeling as you? Do you think that now I have regained my wealth, I would turn my back on Alice simply because I might choose someone better? Can you not understand that there is no one better than your daughter?"

"That is nothing but sentimental nonsense." Lord Blackford waved one hand, dismissing William's words. "In all matters of life, there is never any need for sentiment. I am sure that if you give it a little more thought you will see that my suggestion is very wise indeed."

"You may think so, but then again, I also believe that you have no understanding of what it is like to be in love."

Lord Blackford's eyes flared and, the next moment he broke into such raucous laughter that William's face burned with both fury and outrage.

"You are speaking with such a determined expression that I feel as though I should applaud you for your well thought out drama. You play a part very well, Lord Foster! What is it that you truly seek? There is something binding you to my daughter, and if you do not tell me what it is, then I cannot help you. I will offer you whatever it is you require for you to separate yourself from her forever."

His hands curled into fists as the urge to strike Lord Blackford grew, for what he had said about Alice, for the insults he had laid upon her, and for the sheer disregard towards her, but with an effort, he stayed his hands.

"There is nothing I can say that will make you understand." Getting to his feet, William looked down at the gentleman, seeing the hard planes of his face and the deep, harsh lines. This was not a man with an ounce of kindness in him. "You are a gentleman without emotions. In fact, I believe that you have made your heart so hard that you cannot even *begin* to recognize what I am speaking of. I talk of love, and you mock me. I tell you I am bound to Alice, and you believe me jesting, state that there must be something else I desire from you before I will willingly turn aside. Can you have so little understanding?" Lord Blackford opened his mouth, but William was not finished. "I pity you, Blackford. I pity you because you will never experience what I do at present. You will never understand what it is to love another soul. This is more than just emotion. It is more than mere respect. It is a giving of oneself to another. It is losing an hour, a day, a night, simply because you cannot stop thinking about that person. It is a feeling of being broken apart when they are far from you, but then being fused back together when they are with you. It is a clinging to one's promise, no matter what difficulties may come to pass. It is trusting them with your whole heart and knowing the privilege of being offered their heart in return." Flinging out one arm towards the door, he lifted his chin, fire burning in his eyes. "You may take your leave. I will not hear another word of this."

"You are a fool. My daughter is worth nothing!"

William's jaw tightened, every muscle tense.

"She is my own heart. I fully intend to wed her and to love her every day of my life. I shall bring her a happiness that she has never known before, and it shall be the most beautiful, blessed life for both of us." He took a small step closer, dropping his voice low. "And perhaps one day, you will find yourself looking at us and wondering what it would have been like if you had ever allowed yourself to feel."

The gentleman seemed pinned to his chair in astonishment, for he stared at William with such shock in his expression that his skin turned pale, and it seemed as though he could not find any strength. William did not move, his hand still held out towards the door, and eventually, Lord Blackford slowly rose from his chair. Without a single word, or even a glance toward William, he left the room, and William made sure to close the door tightly behind him.

EPILOGUE

"It did no good."

The drawn curtains hid Alice from her parents as they walked into the library, unwittingly intruding on her solace. They were clearly unaware of where Alice was, and she had no intention of revealing herself either.

"What do you mean?" Her mother's voice was a little higher than usual. "I thought you were to offer him –"

"You do not understand. No matter what I offered him, the gentleman was quite unwilling to step away from Alice. He told me plainly that he would not have it."

Alice's toes curled at the silence which followed. Plainly, her mother was in a great deal of shock that a gentleman such as Lord Foster would not be swayed to turn away from what had been a practical betrothal.

"Then what are we to do? Your sister is expecting Alice to join her very soon."

"I do not think... I do not think that such a thing can take place. We must find another alternative. Alice will wed Lord Foster."

Alice's eyes widened at the gloom in her father's voice. She did not think she had ever heard him so defeated.

"And what explanation will you give? What will you say to your sister about why she cannot have her expected companion?"

Closing her eyes at her mother's harsh tone, Alice leaned her head back against the wall. Even now, at this moment, it seemed she cared more for her sister-in-law's situation in losing Alice as her companion than about Alice herself.

"I shall have to tell her the truth." Even her father sounded heavy-hearted, as if losing a daughter to the hand of a Viscount was a dreadful thing indeed. "I shall have to inform her that our daughter is to marry Lord Foster and that there was nothing I could do to prevent it. Lord Foster himself is quite ridiculous, of course. His explanation and reasons for refusing to end the betrothal made very little sense to me. Personally, I think him a little addled."

Pulling up her knees, Alice dropped her forehead to them and wrapped her arms around her legs. Even in the face of her parents' disappointment at her forthcoming marriage, she could not help her joy. She was to marry Lord Foster and become Viscountess Foster. Nothing was to stand in her way, not even her own father.

"Why? Whatever did he say? We cannot allow our daughter to marry a madman!"

Rolling her eyes, Alice kept her head forward, listening intently.

"He said that he loved her." Lord Blackford's voice crackled with indignation. "Have you ever heard of such foolishness?"

Alice's heart burst into such a furious rhythm that she had to squeeze her eyes closed and clamp her mouth shut for fear that she would exclaim aloud. Yes, they had shared a kiss, but as yet he had not offered her any declaration of his heart. It now seemed that Lord Foster felt more for her than he had been able to express.

"That is utterly ridiculous. There must be something we can do!"

"There is not."

Alice closed her eyes at the sound of her father's defeat, joy lifting her heart. There was to be more happiness in her life than ever before. Everything in her wanted to jump down from the library window, leave the house at once, and make her way directly towards Lord Foster's house, but instead, she chose to remain silent and hidden. Her parents continued to discuss the matter for a few more minutes before finally departing the library, leaving Alice alone, lost in happiness and relief. Tears filled her eyes and she let them fall, filled with an astonishing hope for a promise that she knew would never be broken.

"My dear." Lord Foster's hands reached out to her, her fingers twining through his as she held fast to him. "I have been longing to see you."

"And I you."

Tears burned, but she swallowed hard, not wanting him to know the reason behind them. Not yet at least, for there was so much that she wanted to express first.

"Our wedding is to take place in only a fortnight. I cannot wait for you to become my bride. My love–" Lord Foster broke off suddenly, his eyes flaring wide. Alice said nothing, smiling gently as she looked into his face. He was blinking rapidly, and his chest rose and fell as he took a deep breath. "That is to say," Lord Foster continued. "It is to say that I have found my love for you growing with every day that we have shared thus far." His shoulders dropped as he sighed, letting out a breath of relief that he had been able to speak so openly to her. "That is the truth, Alice. It is not only practicality that binds us together any longer. It is not because of our bargain, not because I am bound to keep to our arrangement. It is because I have fallen in love with you."

"Oh..."

One hand lifted free of hers and ran lightly across her cheek, his fingers trailing from the back of her neck along the curve of her jaw. They were standing together in the shadowy corner of Lord Appleton's ballroom and yet it was as though no one else was present. She could see nothing but Lord Foster, could hear nothing but his voice.

"It is because I love you, and I want us to wed. Nothing would turn me from you now. I have such hope for our future that I believe would have surpassed any financial difficulty. You must know, Alice, that I intend to spend every day of my life making certain that you are aware of just how much I have come to love you."

Heedless to those around her, Alice wrapped her arms around his neck and pulled herself close, smiling up into his eyes.

"I never once expected anything like this, Lord Foster."

A broad grin settled on his lips.

"Nor did I. But now that it has happened, I am so very grateful for it. Grateful for you."

"I know that my father tried to convince you to forget about our betrothal." Catching his eyes widening, she smiled softly. "It does not come as a surprise to me to hear that he did such a thing – but to learn that you would not be convinced to end our betrothal has turned my heart towards you all the more. It is the first time that someone has ever seen me for who I truly am, the first time that someone has valued me for more than how I appear outwardly. I cannot help but love you. I cannot help but find my heart drawing itself to yours, longing to be close to you forever."

Lord Foster dropped his head and kissed her long and hard. Alice leaned into him all the more, his arms around her and her hands around his neck, brushing the edge of his hair. Between their lips came a promise of happiness that they both knew would endure for the rest of their days.

Best wishes for Lord Foster and Alice! They went through so many obstacles to recover his fortune and be together forever!

Check out the next book in the Lost Fortunes, Found Love series For Richer, For Poorer Read ahead a few pages for a sneak peek!

MY DEAR READER

Thank you for reading and supporting my books! I hope this story brought you some escape from the real world into the always captivating Regency world. A good story, especially one with a happy ending, just brightens your day and makes you feel good! If you enjoyed the book, would you leave a review on Amazon? Reviews are always appreciated.

Below is a complete list of all my books! Why not click and see if one of them can keep you entertained for a few hours?

The Duke's Daughters Series
The Duke's Daughters: A Sweet Regency Romance Boxset
A Rogue for a Lady
My Restless Earl
Rescued by an Earl
In the Arms of an Earl
The Reluctant Marquess (Prequel)

A Smithfield Market Regency Romance
The Smithfield Market Romances: A Sweet Regency
Romance Boxset
The Rogue's Flower
Saved by the Scoundrel
Mending the Duke
The Baron's Malady

The Returned Lords of Grosvenor Square
The Returned Lords of Grosvenor Square: A Regency
Romance Boxset
The Waiting Bride
The Long Return
The Duke's Saving Grace
A New Home for the Duke

The Spinsters Guild
The Spinsters Guild: A Sweet Regency Romance Boxset
A New Beginning
The Disgraced Bride
A Gentleman's Revenge
A Foolish Wager
A Lord Undone

Convenient Arrangements
Convenient Arrangements: A Regency Romance
Collection
A Broken Betrothal
In Search of Love
Wed in Disgrace
Betrayal and Lies
A Past to Forget
Engaged to a Friend

Landon House
Landon House: A Regency Romance Boxset
Mistaken for a Rake
A Selfish Heart
A Love Unbroken
A Christmas Match
A Most Suitable Bride

An Expectation of Love

Second Chance Regency Romance
Second Chance Regency Romance Boxset
Loving the Scarred Soldier
Second Chance for Love
A Family of her Own
A Spinster No More

Soldiers and Sweethearts
Soldiers and Sweethearts: A Sweet Regency Romance
Boxset
To Trust a Viscount
Whispers of the Heart
Dare to Love a Marquess
Healing the Earl
A Lady's Brave Heart

Ladies on their Own: Governesses and Companions
More Than a Companion
The Hidden Governess
The Companion and the Earl
More than a Governess
Protected by the Companion
A Wager with a Viscount

Lost Fortunes, Found Love
A Viscount's Stolen Fortune
For Richer, For Poorer

Christmas Stories

Christmas Kisses (Series)

The Lady's Christmas Kiss

Love and Christmas Wishes: Three Regency Romance
Novellas
A Family for Christmas
Mistletoe Magic: A Regency Romance
Heart, Homes & Holidays: A Sweet Romance Anthology

Happy Reading!

All my love,

Rose

A SNEAK PEEK OF FOR
RICHER, FOR POORER

CHAPTER ONE

"It is as bad as we feared, my Lord." Upon hearing those words, Benjamin Harwood, Earl of Wiltsham, rubbed one hand across his eyes, trying to push aside the worry which had been his constant companion these last few weeks. "Come next month, you shall have very little coin with which to pay your staff. You can retain them for another six weeks at the very most, I should imagine."

"Thank you. I appreciate your brutal honesty." Benjamin looked up and gave a small smile to his man of business. "I do not think that I would have been able to see matters so clearly if it had not been for your hard work."

"And as I come to that..." Mr. Crawley looked away. "I do not think that you can employ me for much longer either. You will have to make a great many changes when it comes to your way of living, my Lord. Perhaps it is time that I seek out another employer."

Benjamin scowled.

"I am determined to employ you for as long as it is possible. I have found my valet new employment rather than lose you. These last few weeks I have only managed to keep myself afloat because of your work!"

"Might I ask?" Again, Mr. Crawley's gaze darted away as he rubbed his hands together. There was a seriousness in this discussion that could not be escaped. Benjamin nodded, and Crawley went on. "I want to ask what your intentions are, my Lord. Do you intend to remain at your estate? Or have you any thought about returning to London?"

A cold sensation ran over Benjamin's frame, and he shivered.

"I have very little intention of returning to London. If I can, I shall remain here and make as many economies as I can – and am I not saving expense if I remain here rather than take the carriage to London? An Earl can hardly be seen in London without his carriage!"

A carriage which I can ill afford at present.

A flicker of a smile caught the man's lips.

"Yes, my Lord, you are. I ask only because I have heard from a friend back in London, who states that your acquaintance, Lord Foster, is well on his way to recovering his fortune. He has a great deal of hope, I believe."

Benjamin's breath caught in his chest as he stared at Mr. Crawley. He had not heard from Lord Foster in some days, but could it truly be that the man was soon to regain his fortune? He knew that Lord Foster had been absolutely determined to do so, but if he was close to succeeding, then that gave Benjamin a little hope as regarded his circumstances.

"Are you sure?"

"I can assure you it is quite true. You know that I am not a man inclined towards gossip. I tell you this so that you might find a little encouragement."

"I am glad to hear of it, for such news may change things a little," Benjamin mused. "I shall write to Lord Foster this very afternoon so that I can hear from him what steps he has taken thus far."

"Then you may return to London after all?"

"I may. I am certain that the *ton* would not be glad of my return, however. I am quite sure that there are more than a few rumors flying about me."

His wry smile was met with silence from Mr. Crawley, which caused Benjamin to wince. Evidently that was true.

"If I may be clear, my Lord, returning to London to seek to regain your fortune is the only way that you can ever return to your previous way of living. As it stands at present, you are a most impoverished gentleman and that will bring with it a great many difficulties."

"Yes, I am well aware of that." So saying, Benjamin pinched the bridge of his nose. "I shall write to Lord Foster this afternoon and I will keep you informed as to whether or not I plan to return to London."

His man of business rose to his feet.

"I am very sorry, my Lord, for all that you have struggled with these last few weeks. The situation itself sounds greatly disturbing."

"I thank you. It is a relief to be believed, at least. I know that you are doing everything you can to aid me with my situation of poverty, as it stands thus far."

"A situation which we must hope we can change, my Lord."

And with that, Mr. Crawley took his leave and Benjamin sat entirely alone, as he had been for so long. Leaning forward, he rested his elbows on his knees and dropped his head into his hands for a moment, struggling not to give in to despair. It had long threatened him, but as yet he was doing a somewhat acceptable job of managing to ignore its lingering presence.

He reached to ring the bell, in the hope of asking his butler or one of the maids for something a little stronger to drink, only to recall that he had no whisky nor brandy left in the house. He had already been forced to make careful decisions as regarded his present circumstances. An impoverished gentleman could not have such things as the very best brandy and thus he had been forced to economize. It had brought him great pain, of course, but what was to be done? As things stood, his situation was very difficult indeed, and he was close to giving up all hope.

Rising from his chair, he wandered to the window and looked out upon his estate. Was he truly to be the one who would ruin his family situation entirely? Was his name to bear the disgrace of their poverty for generations to come? At times, he wanted to weep over what had occurred, only to remind himself that he had not caused it deliberately. If it was as Lord Foster stated, then it appeared that he had not been responsible for his actions that fateful evening. Not that the *ton* would believe it, however, and their opinion would mean that life in London would be rather difficult indeed.

But I must, I shall go.

Speaking determinedly to himself, Benjamin allowed himself a little sense of hope. Mayhap if Lord Foster was able to recover his fortune, then did not that give him a chance to do the same? Out of the six gentlemen who had been injured that evening, Lord Foster had been the most determined to recover everything and to understand what had taken place.

"Perhaps he has been successful."

Mumbling to himself, Benjamin drew his fingers

through his hair, sending it awry, but he did not care. He had spoken to no one other than his staff these last few weeks, and certainly no one had come to call upon him. Why would they do so now, when they knew him to be impoverished; when there was a scandal attached to his name? Mr. Crawley was correct. There was very little hope for him or his family name unless he could find a way to recover his fortune, and remove himself from this situation of poverty, once and for all.

Resting his hands on the windowsill, Benjamin leaned forward, let out a long breath and let his head dangle. That ill-fated evening had been a very difficult one indeed. He had awoken the following day with a concerned butler standing over him with news of his evident foolishness in a letter written by his solicitors at a most early hour. With horror, Benjamin had learned that he had signed a contract, giving his fortune over to a gentleman of whom he had no knowledge. What was worse, was that he had the name of such a fellow, but when he came to look for him, he could find neither hide nor hair of the man. The name, he assumed, was false, but the fortune, however, was gone.

And all because we did as Lord Gillespie suggested and made our way to the East End of London instead of playing at our usual gambling dens.

He could not recall a single thing about that evening. it was nothing more than darkness that shrouded his mind, refusing to give him clarity no matter how hard he begged for it. The last he recalled, he had been enjoying a game of poker, but after that, there came nothing else. Somehow, in the depths of confusion, he had decided to give his fortune away in its entirety and thus had left himself almost completely penniless. At least he had not been the only one affected, or else he would have been quite lost in despair.

Not only Lord Foster, but five other gentlemen were also in such a situation, having each lost their fortunes that dark night. However, all but Lord Foster had returned to their estates, with Lord Stoneleigh needing to recover from an injury sustained that evening. The rest had disappeared, ashamed, and uncertain as to what else they were to do. The *ton* was no longer their friend, turning its back on them entirely. After all, what could an impoverished gentleman offer any of the young ladies of the *ton*, other than a creeping, grasping eagerness for their dowries? Even the thought of returning to London sent a sharp coldness through Benjamin's frame.

"My Lord, you have a letter."

Benjamin turned sharply, just as his butler came into the room. He had already been forced to reduce the number of servants in his home, but those who remained, he very much wished to retain for as long as he could. *But Mr. Crawley stated that I can only afford them for another six weeks at the most.*

"I thank you. Wait a moment until I see if it requires a response."

Opening up the letter, he read the brief lines quickly. His heart soared high, exploding with a sudden, furious hope which seemed to lend a fresh brightness to the room, his breath catching swiftly.

"There is no reply needed, but you must make my carriage ready at once."

"Your carriage, my Lord?"

"Yes. I shall pack my things and depart within the hour." His voice grew a little higher as he hurried towards the door, leaving the butler to stand in the middle of the room. "I am to go to London, and I have every hope of returning with my fortune restored and my estate once more secure."

He did not wait for the butler's response, but pulled the door closed and hurried towards his rooms, fully aware that he would have to pack his own things, given that he had no servant to do it. That did not seem to matter much any longer, however. Lord Foster's letter begged for him to return to London, telling him that he had found a way forward. Now, there was nothing that Benjamin wanted to do other than make his way directly to London so that he might aid Lord Foster in the recovery of his fortune and, in turn, find a little light of hope for himself.

CHAPTER TWO

"So you are now in your second Season, Julia."

Miss Julia Carshaw lifted her head from her book, a book which she had been pretending to read while her brother had stalked through their London townhouse looking for things to complain about. She had no doubt that one of his complaints would be her. Ever since he had taken on the title a little over three years ago, he had become increasingly irritable, with high demands and nothing short of perfection required.

Julia was well aware that she was nowhere near close to perfection. Not that such a thing mattered to her, of course, but it did to her brother, and she was expected to do a great deal better than she was at present.

"Julia. Are you paying me any heed whatsoever?"

"Yes, brother."

Julia closed her book completely as if to show that she was giving him her full attention. Not that she had any intention at all of giving any true thought to whatever it was he was about to throw at her, but the outward appearance of it would be required to placate him.

"As I have previously told you, you are in your second Season and that is something of a disappointment to me. I had expected you to wed already."

Julia's lips twitched.

"I am afraid that I cannot speak for the lack of suitable gentlemen in London last Season."

"Pshaw!" Her brother's guttural exclamation threw aside her weak excuse. "That is nonsense, Julia. You know as well as I that there were many gentlemen interested in your company last Season, but that you refused to acknowledge any of them. Indeed, did not Lord Comfrey seek to acquaint himself with you? He very much wished to court you, did he not?" A dark frown pulled at her brother's forehead. "At least for a time anyway."

Julia forced her lips to remain very flat indeed. Lord Comfrey had indeed offered to court her, but Julia had quickly dissuaded him of such a desire by behaving in a manner he found most inappropriate. Lord Comfrey expected young ladies to stand quite silently, share none of their opinions, and only smile as a singular expression of their enjoyment of any occasion. Julia, on the other hand, had made certain to laugh uproariously, speak her opinion without it having been requested, and talk at length about her love of horses when Lord Comfrey had already stated that it ought to be a discussion saved for the gentlemen only. Lord Comfrey had withdrawn his eagerness to court her soon afterwards - much to her brother's frustration, of course.

"You will find a husband for yourself, Julia. You shall find him within the next fortnight."

Julia's mouth fell open.

"A - a fortnight, brother?" Stuttering, she threw up her

hands. "That is ridiculous. I cannot find a suitable husband in two weeks! The Season has not long begun."

Viscount Kingston rose to his full height, pulling his shoulders back, and glaring at her as though she had displeased him by speaking so.

"Nevertheless, I have decided it shall be a fortnight. And if you do not Julia, then I have every intention of finding you a husband myself."

The confidence and courage which had been in Julia's soul quickly faded, crumpling away into nothing. Her brother's demands were entirely unfair. He could not expect her to find a husband within a fortnight. Surely that was not the done thing, and would raise many an eyebrow should she find herself in such a position. The *ton* would take note of her haste, and wonder why she was doing such a thing.

Perhaps I can use such reasons to my advantage.

"The *ton* will note such eagerness, brother. They might suggest that –"

"I care not for your excuses!"

"It is not excuses, brother." Rising from her chair, Julia took a step towards him, seeing his eyebrows dropping lower still. The last few years had proven to her that her brother was not particularly fond of her, but she had not thought that he disliked her as much as this! "Our family name will be stained if you demand such a thing of me. There will be whispers long after I am wed, which may well cause you difficulty with finding your own match when the time comes."

She wanted to rail at him, to state that it was unfair of him to demand such a thing of her when he was unwed, but carefully held herself back. There is no need to antagonize him still further.

Viscount Kingston folded his arms across his chest, his eyebrows falling still lower over his eyes until all she could see was darkness in his face. Something within her trembled, but she did not back away, resolved not to do as he said. Instead, she kept her chin lifted and her eyes steady, refusing to be cowed.

"Again, you give me excuses, Julia."

"I give you no such thing. I speak the truth. I am not the only young lady in London who did not wed after their first Season. There will be many of us here for our second Season. Why do you place such demands on me? They are most unfair. Even a month would be a difficult request, but it would be better than a fortnight."

Her brother refused to give her any explanation whatsoever.

"I shall find you a husband, one way or the other, Julia. You have a fortnight."

"I shall not wed whoever it is you choose for me."

She was aware that she was speaking foolishly now, but her resolve to disabuse her brother of any notion of control was strong and forced her tongue into action.

Viscount Kingston chuckled, low and dark.

"I think you forget, sister, that I am the one who holds the purse strings. I shall have order in this family. I shall have decorum and I shall have a sister who is wed and settled so that she can no longer be a constant burden on my daily life, on my time, and on my finances." Julia reared back, horrified by her brother's sudden vehemence. She had always known that he was a selfish creature, but she had never thought, nor heard it, to such an extent as this. Her chest grew tight and painful, her breathing difficult. "You shall wed, Julia. I will make sure of it." The only thing she could do was shake her head in refusal. "Yes, you shall."

Struggling to find her voice, Julia forced her gaze up towards her brother.

"I will not marry whoever you choose for me. I do not care how suitable you may think they are, I will *not* have my choice made for me. You may force me to the altar, but I shall never say the words which will tie me to a gentleman for the rest of my life. Not unless *I* can choose the gentleman."

Her brother laughed, shaking his head.

"Do you truly believe that you have any control here? Julia, what shall you do, if you do not wed? Do you have any resources of your own which would permit you to do such a thing?" His words mocked her, and Julia's skin prickled, her heart beginning to pound. This was not at all what she had expected. "Either you will wed, or you will become a spinster and I shall send you to someone who can make more use of you than I can." Julia shook her head, mute. There was nothing she could say. "I shall give you a month, as you have so demanded, but only out of the kindness of my heart. Otherwise, my dear sister, you will find yourself in church with the gentleman whom I select, and then you will have a choice to make. Either you will marry him, and thereby find a life of comfort and all that is good, or you will choose to become a spinster with no money, no good standing, and no future. The choice shall be yours."

Without another word, he strode from the room, leaving Julia breathless with shock and fear as she sank into her chair. Yes, her brother had become much more irritable these last few years, but she had never expected him to demand such a thing as this of her.

I have only a month.

The thought was a terrifying one. How could she have so little time in which she must find herself a suitable gentleman, else face the wrath of her brother? Would he really be as cruel as to force her into spinsterhood? Her stomach twisted as she acknowledged that yes, he would do so. Evidently, she had been a burden upon him for too long. She had known nothing of this, not until this very moment, but it now seemed that her brother had no wish to keep her in his company any longer. He did not wish to pay for her gowns, for her pin money, or for the fripperies that she rarely enjoyed. It appeared that her brother wanted only to consider himself.

"What am I to do?"

Murmuring to herself, Julia rose from her seat and made her way across the room. The London Season had not been particularly enjoyable thus far, but that was mostly due to the fact that she had very little time for the London gentlemen who cared nothing for her and sought only her dowry. She sought a husband who would show an interest in her company, who wished to hear what she had to say, and who had a kind character. All too aware that such a thing was a rarity for any gentleman in London, Julia squeezed her eyes closed and fought despair. She was stronger than this, was she not? Yes, her brother had demanded it, and in doing so, had astonished her entirely, but when had she ever done as her brother asked? That was one of the reasons for his irritation. To her mind, he was not her father, and thus could not make the same demands as a father might.

And father would have been a good deal more considerate, I am sure.

A single tear slipped onto her cheek as she looked down at the London street. There was very little here that brought her any sense of happiness. Yes, there was pleasant company, but she had struggled to find any particular friendship with any young lady from the previous Season. The young ladies were much too eager to discuss dresses and the latest fashion, which Julia did not find of interest, and gentlemen, on the whole, had no desire to hear what a young lady such as herself had to say. A dreadful fear suddenly took hold of her, squeezing her breath from her lungs. What if she could find no particular man to be her husband? If the *ton* was as difficult as all that, then surely the chance of her finding a gentleman whom she considered truly respectable and kind would be nigh on impossible!

Then I shall be a spinster.

Her bottom lip wobbled a little as she drew in a deep breath, telling herself that she was not about to give in to tears.

"Spinsterhood cannot be so terrible a situation, I am sure."

Her confident words did nothing to ease the pain in her heart. Try as she might, she could not pretend that being a spinster was anything more than a dreadful prospect. She would have no happiness. No doubt she would be required to find a situation where she might be able to support herself one way or the other, but quite how she was to go about that, Julia did not know. She had no skills with which to do such a thing as that, and if her brother were to find the situation for her, then Julia had every belief that it would not be a pleasant one. He would do whatever he could to punish her for not doing as he had demanded of her, in finding a husband.

"He has all of the control."

Resting her head lightly against the cool glass of the windowpane, Julia closed her eyes. What was a young lady such as herself to do in this situation? Her brother held the purse strings, and he had every opportunity to demand such things of her, knowing that she could do nothing other than either agree or face the consequences of refusing.

Then perhaps I shall have to do something quite extraordinary.

Julia lifted her chin and set her shoulders, refusing to allow any more tears to fall. Yes, her brother had always protested that she was most frustrating when it came to the fact that *she* would do as she thought best rather than pay heed to his own opinion, but now Julia was glad that she had done so. It meant that she had the courage and the fortitude to find her own path, regardless of whatever blocks he put in her way. He would not be successful in this. She would find her own way forward, in one manner or another.

And she would begin this very evening.

WHAT WILL JULIA DO? Something extraordinary! I hope it works out for her! Check out the rest of the story in the Kindle store For Richer, For Poorer

JOIN MY MAILING LIST

Sign up for my newsletter to stay up to date on new releases, contests, giveaways, freebies, and deals!

Free book with signup!

Facebook Giveaways! Books and Amazon gift cards! Join me on Facebook: https://www. facebook.com/rosepearsonauthor

Join my new Facebook group! Rose's Ravenous Readers

Website: www.RosePearsonAuthor.com

Follow me on Goodreads: Author Page

You can also follow me on Bookbub! Click on the picture below – see the Follow button?

Printed in Great Britain
by Amazon

25484696R00116